Village Affairs

TRIPLE INTENT

KRISTIAN PARKER

Triple Intent
ISBN # 978-1-80250-989-2
©Copyright Kristian Parker 2022
Cover Art by Kelly Martin ©Copyright October 2022
Interior text design by Claire Siemaszkiewicz
Pride Publishing

Pride Publishing books by Kristian Parker

Speak Its Name
To Light a Fire
Call it Love
Spotlight on Love

Village Affairs
The Rule of Three
Three's Company
Triple Intent

Collections
My Bloody Valentine: Venetian Valentine
Sun, Sea and Spotted Squid

TRIPLE INTENT

Dedication

This is for Rebecca, the best editor in the whole of
the land. Thank you for everything that you do.
Knitters rule!

Chapter One

Even in December, the Greek sunlight streamed through a chink in the curtains, painting the bed in heat. François Vernier stretched out in the Egyptian cotton sheets and tried to ignore the dull thud of a hangover playing in his brain. They had started the party early, yet it felt like he'd only just put his head down.

A very disorientated Darryl Burlington emerged from under the duvet with a lop-sided grin. "Merry Christmas, François."

The nausea came rapidly, and François had to lay his head on the pillow again. "*Joyeux Noel.*"

Darryl plumped his pillows and sat up. "What a night, eh?"

François nodded. "I need coffee. You want?"

Not waiting for a reply, he got out of bed and padded over to the kitchen area of the vast suite Darryl had taken where he made himself busy grinding some beans. The view down to the Ionian Sea took his breath away and once the machine bubbled into life, he took it all in.

Kefalonia was a small island on the west coast of Greece. François had been to many other Greek islands but never this one. He couldn't wait to return in the summer when it would be warm enough to dive into those blue waters. François prided himself on always being a participant and hated being a spectator.

Ever impatient, he waited until just enough coffee for two cups had brewed. Filling them, he ignored the hissing sound of more dripping onto the hot plate.

He went through to the bedroom. Darryl hadn't moved. As fresh as a daisy, he grinned at him. Darryl believed hangovers were for the weak. François didn't dare glance in the mirror that covered half a wall. But Darryl had insisted on partying into the night so he would have to take him as he found him.

"What are we doing today?" Darryl asked.

François handed him his cup and opened the curtains a little. He didn't care if anyone saw him naked. It would give them an early Christmas treat. He'd been turning heads since he'd been in his pram. His mother told him that when she'd pushed him through town, people would stop and speak to him. If they were lucky, he would reward them with a smile. Some days he wouldn't.

He blew on his coffee and took a sip. The hangover had become a little more insistent, and he regretted making quite so many plans for today. "George said he would take us out on the boat. Everywhere is closed, so I thought a picnic somewhere lovely then back here for dinner."

Darryl nodded.

François went over to his bag that lay on the chair. He rummaged inside and retrieved the gift he had kept secret. "Merry Christmas."

He handed it to a surprised Darryl. "I thought we weren't doing gifts. I haven't got you anything."

François shrugged and ignored the feeling in his heart. Darryl ripped off the paper and revealed the monogrammed leather notebook from Aspinal.

"Oh, François. I love it. Thank you."

Darryl reached out his hand for François. He sat down on the bed, and they hugged each other awkwardly.

"Ah you're awake. I thought you two were going to sleep all of Christmas Day."

François spun round to see Ezio, the Greek barman they had picked up the night before. He stood in the doorway wearing just a towel. His thick curly hair dripped water onto his furry chest, the inviting glint in his eye that had first prompted Darryl to send François over with their indecent proposal still very much in place.

"François?" Darryl said, licking his lips. "Tell George not to bother with the boat. I think we should stay at home today."

He pulled the duvet aside, letting the notebook fall to the floor. François glanced momentarily at the gift lying there before putting on his game face.

"Yes, boss. Sounds good to me."

Ezio dropped the towel, revealing the delights they had enjoyed all night long. François' cock twitched. Darryl probably had a point. A day on the high seas would only make him seasick. He walked over and kissed Ezio.

"That's right, boys," Darryl said. He put his hands behind his head, licking his lips. "Give me a Christmas show."

* * * *

Four hours later, they had moved onto champagne. Ezio had some stamina on him. François lay on the couch, sipping a glass as he listened to Darryl and Ezio going at it in the next room.

If his parents could see him now, he didn't know if they would be impressed or disgusted. Probably a mix of the two. He hadn't spoken to them in ten years so who knew?

The suite had everything he and Darryl could want. A private pool, butler—who Darryl had magnanimously given the day off—and wraparound views. His mind rested on the Christmas Days he'd had as a kid. His grandparents coming to see his new toys and playing simple games before joining the rest of the village for carols.

A tear escaped his eye which he hastily wiped away. *No use dwelling on the past.*

Draining the glass, he wandered over to the wine cooler and grabbed another bottle. There was always another when he travelled with Darryl Burlington.

He made his way over to the bedroom, to be greeted by the sight of Ezio riding Darryl's cock hard. His lithe furry body bucked in time to Darryl's grunting. François popped the cork loudly and they both stopped.

"I thought you might need some refreshment."

Ezio climbed off Darryl, pulling the condom off him and throwing it in the bin. "Sounds good to me," he replied.

Darryl hadn't left the bed yet. Why would he? Everything had been brought to him.

François poured the champagne and handed a long-stemmed crystal flute to each of the sweating men.

"What time did you say you were working, Ezio?"

Sipping his drink, the gorgeous man glanced at his watch.

"Oh shit," he exclaimed. He slammed the glass down on the bedside table. "Can I have another shower?"

"Sure," Darryl said.

Ezio brushed past François and out of the room.

"He can go on forever," Darryl grinned.

"You weren't doing so bad yourself," François replied.

At forty-two years old, Darryl Burlington was still in his prime. Sweat beaded on his dark brown skin as he took a swig of his drink. "I'm starving," he announced. "Get rid of him and we can go for dinner?"

François tried not to pout. "I thought we could order up and watch a movie."

Darryl shook his head. "Nah, that'll be boring. Let's see if there's any life going on out there. Maybe find us one last Christmas treat?" He winked at François.

"You're on heat," he said.

"It's Christmas Day." Darryl laughed. "What are we doing tomorrow?"

François walked over to the window. "George is taking us to the site in the morning. Then our flight is at two."

"Perfect. I might have a quick nap. Build my strength up."

Darryl snuggled down under the sheets. François drained his glass and walked out to the living area where Ezio had thrown on a pair of jeans.

"Do you know what happened to my T-shirt?" he said.

François took him in. Another exceptionally handsome man to add to their collection. He couldn't say he hadn't enjoyed being fucked all ways by him. But he joined a very long line. Darryl was a hunter and soon lost interest when the quarry was captured.

François dug behind one of the sofa cushions and found a grey T-shirt. He threw it across to the gorgeous man.

"Thanks," Ezio said with a wink. "I had a really great time."

"Yeah, me too," François said.

He always had to the get rid of them. No matter how many people they invited to the room, François assumed the role of doorman. They would always want more, and he would have to let them down gently. Darryl probably didn't even know this dance was done after he'd had his pleasure.

"Do you want to tell your face that?" Ezio said.

"Huh?"

"It's Christmas Day, François. You look as though you're going to the dentist."

François smiled. "Sorry. Been working hard lately."

Pulling the shirt over his head, Ezio came over and wrapped his arms around François' waist. He ignored the instinct to push him away.

"Now you've played hard. It's the best medicine." Ezio kissed him. "Should I say goodbye to Darryl?"

François shook his head. "Best not. He's getting some shut-eye before we get to do it all again."

"Call in at the bar?" Ezio asked hopefully.

François nodded vaguely. Darryl didn't believe in lightning striking twice, so they wouldn't be going in that bar again.

"Sure. Now go to work," he said. He extracted himself from Ezio's arms and walked over to the hallway. "I'm going to finish that bottle and find a trashy Christmas movie to watch."

But Ezio didn't move. "Why don't you just be with him?"

François stopped in his tracks. "I'm sorry?"

"Darryl. It's obvious you're in love with him."

Tension ran through François' body. Ezio wasn't the first to say this, but the question always made him defensive. It must be crystal clear for people on the outside. "It's not that like that. Darryl and I are complicated."

Ezio made a face. "I can't see how. When I've gone, go in there and fuck his brains out. Then tell him you love him."

François dashed over to the open bedroom door. The room lay in darkness, but surely Darryl couldn't have dropped off that quickly. He did not want him overhearing this stranger dissecting a relationship they had never bothered to define in eight years. He gently shut the door.

"Firstly, we only play with others. Secondly, I'm not in love with anyone, thank you. Thirdly, if I were I wouldn't be discussing it with a stranger. Got that?"

Realising he would have to be way more forthright, he marched over to the main door. Opening it with purpose, he wanted to make it perfectly clear this experience had come to an end. But Ezio wasn't so easily put off. He stopped by François, his face so close that François could smell the stale alcohol on him.

"Will you return to Kefalonia?"

"Probably," François said. "We're thinking of buying a place in the south. I will come for the opening."

"Then get in touch."

"Darryl probably won't come. He doesn't bother these days."

"I don't care. I'd like to see you again."

This man had outstayed his welcome. His overconfident manner grated on François. "Sure, whatever. Find me on Insta. François Vernier."

Ezio nodded and kissed him before leaving the suite. François shut the door behind him. He did not need to be psychoanalysed by a one-night stand on Christmas Day. *When did meaningless sex become such hard work?*

Resisting the temptation to crawl in beside Darryl, he sat down on the couch and poured himself another glass of champagne. He didn't blame Ezio for being envious that he lived the high life in suites like this, but he wouldn't let some scheming barman overstep the mark. He had spent the last few years being everything Darryl needed. He knew what he wanted before Darryl did. Darryl often joked that he was more of a husband than an assistant. At night when he was alone in bed, François would think about what it would be like if they were real partners.

We could rule the world.

Chapter Two

The fire roared as the speakers blared out Christmas tunes. For the first time in decades Thorpe Hall, nestled on the outskirts of the tiny Yorkshire village of Napthwaite, rang with laughter and merriment and a tree twinkled in the window.

In the dining room, the members of Thorpe's newest family unit tucked into a Christmas feast. Matthew Johnstone presided over the table as his son, Will, served a succulent turkey with all the trimmings. Will's partners, Andrew and Hardeep, also sat at the table, along with Hardeep's fifteen-year-old daughter, Satinder.

"This is wonderful, Will," Matthew said.

Michael Fleming, next to Satinder, saw Will's face light up at the compliment from his father. They had been through quite a year with Matthew's heart attack and Will returning to the village...and falling in love with Hardeep and Andrew, much to his father's dismay.

Then the strangest thing had happened. Will and Hardeep had put their lives at risk rescuing Andrew from his violent ex. Faced with the prospect of losing his son, Matthew had embraced him for who he was. As Hall gardener, Michael had still witnessed the odd argument, but it had been a joy to watch the father and son rediscover each other.

"Thank you again for inviting me," Michael said as Will put another roast potato onto his plate. He'd been planning a turkey crown for one and falling asleep in front of the Queen's speech. When Will had insisted he join them, Michael hadn't taken much persuading.

"It's the least we could do," Matthew said. "After all your hard work on the garden, you're a member of this community now."

Will winked at Michael. "You must wonder what kind of a village you've moved to, Michael. Gay throuples popping up all over the place."

"That's enough, Will," Matthew said. "We've all learnt to adapt this year, that's a certainty."

"Cheers, everyone," Andrew Norris said. He raised his glass.

"To absent friends," Hardeep Kaur added, his eyes filling with tears. Hardeep had recently lost his mother. She'd gone to visit relatives in India, and he'd received the terrible news that she had died in her sleep. Her heart had given out.

"Your mother will be missed in the village, Hardeep," Matthew said from his seat at the head of the table.

"Thank you."

The roast potato absolutely melted in Michael's mouth. It had been a long time since he'd experienced home cooking like this. "Will, this meal is incredible," he gushed. This set forth a chorus of cooing and compliments.

Will blushed and sat next to his father.

"It feels like a world away from that court room last week," Andrew said.

"How did it go?" Michael asked. "It's ridiculous that you even have to attend. The police saw you'd been attacked."

"I wanted to go to the court," Andrew replied. "The first time it happened, I ran away to this wonderful village. This time, I wanted him to see I'm not scared of him."

"I'm sorry I couldn't come. Will said you were very brave," Matthew said.

"That's okay, I didn't expect you to. I had my two cheerleaders, so nothing could stop me."

Andrew winked across the table at Will and Hardeep, who grinned at him. Ever since the horrible incident with Andrew's ex attacking him, the three had been inseparable. Even the sad news about Hardeep's mother had only served to forge their relationship stronger. Loneliness flooded Michael's system as he witnessed this.

"Then you are very lucky indeed," Matthew stated.

In what seemed like record time, all the serving dishes on the table were emptied and not a solitary brussels sprout remained. Will set about clearing the table, and Michael leapt up to help.

"You're a guest," Will said, slapping his hand.

"I don't care. I'm not letting you do all the work."

"We should all pitch in," Hardeep said.

"We do have a dishwasher, you know," Will replied.

Michael stacked the plates expertly, clearing all six and some serving dishes.

"And we have a professional in our midst," Andrew added.

"Years of being made to work in my mother's café over the summer finally paid off," Michael replied.

"Where did you grow up, Michael?" Matthew asked.

"Dad, have you never asked him anything about himself?" Will scolded.

Matthew shifted uncomfortably. "I was busy having a heart attack."

"I grew up in Southend-on-Sea," Michael informed him.

"An Essex boy, no less?" Andrew said.

Michael nodded. "And proud of it."

Will had cleared the other dishes. "Satinder, why don't you go and find us a movie to watch. Then we can have pudding. Unless you want it now?" he offered.

Everyone groaned and rubbed their bellies. Satinder dashed into the lounge.

"You know we'll be forced to watch *The Holiday* again," Hardeep told them.

Matthew struggled to his feet. Michael watched him closely. He was getting frailer, but he had an air of contentedness about him that had not been there when Michael had started working here. "Let the girl watch what she likes," he said. "She's done ever so well today."

Andrew rubbed Hardeep's back. "So have you."

Michael followed Will into the kitchen. "Just pile them up there. The dishwasher is on, but I can load it again later."

"Please let me be on dishwasher duties," Michael said.

Will reached into the fridge and brought out a half-drunk bottle of Bollinger. "I know we're technically on the wine now. But waste not, want not, eh? Grab us a couple of glasses out of that cupboard."

Michael perched up on a stool at the kitchen island opposite Will. He held out the glasses, and Will emptied the bottle into them. "Cheers," Michael said for about the hundredth time that day. "What shall we drink to?"

Will took the proffered glass and tapped the tip with Michael's. "To new beginnings."

The spectre of uncertainty crept into Michael's chest.

"You, okay?" Will asked, staring intently at him.

"Yes of course. It just felt a bit sad to see the *Sold* sign when I walked up the path this morning."

Will fiddled with the champagne cork that was lying on the countertop. Michael instantly regretted bringing the subject up. It had been Will's idea for his father to sell the big Hall. They had discussed it over a bottle of wine one night. Will knew he was practically sacking Michael at the same time, but Michael had understood.

"Have you had any more thoughts about what you'll do?"

What will I do? He had been asking himself that for two months since they had announced their intentions.

"Dad says you can stay in the cottage rent-free for as long as you like," Will added.

"I can't expect him to do that."

"Of course, you can. He'll be richer than God when he gets the cash from this place."

"He got a good deal then?"

Will whistled. "A very good deal. Believe me, you won't be sending him to the poor house by staying in the cottage for however long you need."

"Can I ask…? Sorry, no, it's none of my business."

"Go on."

Michael fiddled with the stem of his glass. "Who have you sold to? I understand if it's confidential. I didn't want to put you on the spot. I just wondered."

Will touched his arm. "It's perfectly understandable. We wanted to tell you. They insisted we wait until the contracts were signed. It's the Burlington Hotel Group."

"Caught red-handed manhandling the gardener." Andrew stood in the doorway. "Aren't two handsome men enough for you, Will Johnstone?" He came and put his arm around Will, who cuddled into him. Andrew kissed the top of his head.

"I hope he's not making unreasonable demands on you, Michael."

"Only that he won't let me be in charge of the dishwasher," he replied.

Hardeep came into the kitchen. "Who is squabbling over the dishwasher?"

He came over and slipped his arm around Andrew's waist. Andrew seemed to be bursting with happiness, flanked by his two men. Although happy for them, Michael would be going home to a cold, empty cottage that night. It would be nice to have someone to snuggle with under the duvet.

"Is Satinder all right, do you think?" Will asked.

"Your father is entertaining her with tales of Christmas past. Poor girl."

Michael drained his glass. "I suppose we should save her. I promised your father a game of Scrabble."

"Oh, no. This could spell trouble," Hardeep said.

The protests at his terrible joke only served to put a wider smile on his face. They disentangled themselves from each other, and Michael followed them into the lounge.

Five hours later, and fuller than he thought possible, Michael lay on the sofa in his little cottage, the room lit only by the fairy lights from the tree. The church bells had just chimed midnight. Christmas Day was officially over.

With a glass of brandy on the table next to him and the laptop perched on his alarmingly round belly, he typed *Burlington Hotel Group* into the search engine.

The usual blurb about the various properties they owned came up on the screen. They were a luxury hotel brand with places in London, the South of France, the Algarve and Croatia, amongst other places. They looked like beautifully restored buildings with a high price tag. But Michael wanted to know who ran the show. He clicked the *About* page.

The name *Darryl Burlington* titled the page. The CEO was a stunningly handsome man. Michael read the blurb.

Darryl opened his first hotel in 2001 in the East End of London. He soon went on to open hotels across the globe, bringing his own take on luxury travel to both business and leisure customers alike.

Michael skimmed the rest but couldn't take his eyes off the picture. Something stirred in him.

He typed in *Darryl Burlington* and a whole raft of articles came up. A YouTube video popped up on his machine. Some journalist interviewing Darryl at the Black British Business Awards in 2020.

"Darryl, you've won the award for Entrepreneur. How does that make you feel?" asked the interviewer.

Darryl beamed at the camera. "I can't put it into words. It's no secret that I didn't have the best start in life so to be validated by my peers like this...well, words can't describe it."

"You've been accused of buying up places in little-known locations and decimating the local economy. How do you feel about that?"

Darryl shifted uncomfortably on the screen. "We bring jobs to unknown areas. It would be easy for me to set up in a capital city. I want to discover hidden gems."

Michael shut the screen down and stared at the twinkling lights. Change was coming to Napthwaite. Where would that leave him?

Chapter Three

A few weeks later, Darryl Burlington, the new owner of Thorpe Hall, strode into the dining room. "When is the furniture getting here?"

François frowned at his ever-present iPad. "Later this afternoon. I'm tracking it."

"What are we going to do until then?" Darryl asked, examining the old fireplace that dominated the room. There were still bits of tinsel taped to the mantelpiece. The previous owners had removed everything except a few touches here and there seemingly.

François put the tablet down. "I did suggest we came next week once they'd had a chance to make it habitable."

"Where's the fun in that?" Darryl grinned. "Besides, I want to get a feel for the place." He had been in every room. Thorpe Hall had massive potential. Six big bedrooms and three reception rooms that would form the heart of the hotel.

"This is going to make a great bar," Darryl said, ideas flowing through him. "I want that country-house vibe. Instead of optics and stuff, why don't we put an old wardrobe in that corner? Then it won't feel like a bar. It will be like guests are in their own home. It can have everything in, and we'll get a nice vintage table for service."

François followed where he pointed. "Not a bad idea. Home from home kind of thing. But you're getting ahead of yourself. The building work is going to take months."

"Get your coat, Frankie. Let's go and have a look."

"I hate it when you call me that."

"That's why I do it."

They put on their duck-down jackets, bought especially for this foray into the cold north, and let themselves outside. The gardens appeared to have been split into beds. At the height of January, Darryl couldn't tell what plants lay inside. Not that it would make a difference if they were in full bloom. "Do you have the plans?"

François held up the iPad.

"I can't see shit on that thing. Talk to me." He ignored François' pained expression. After eight years together, he would have thought his ways of working would be obvious.

"Okay," François said, squinting at the screen. "Obviously the space to expand was the selling point here. The house itself will only do so much. The plans have us building over most of these gardens. We can do it sympathetically and get another forty bedrooms, dining room and kitchens. There's no point in doing a pool—it's practically Siberia round here. We keep the lawns and have a separate building for the spa."

Darryl took it all in. "Is it all in budget?"

François tapped on the screen. "Under budget, actually. If we bring it in on time, of course."

He nodded. "I like it. We need to factor in parking too. Take the flower beds at the side."

"You don't want any formal gardens? A lot of work has been done on these."

"Nah, it's not a stately home. Gardens like that are dead space. Keep a tiny bit for a drinks terrace but just pots. We can move them then for any events."

"Sure thing."

Darryl set off toward the house. "I'm starving," he said. They had driven straight from London. He always felt like a child on Christmas morning when getting the keys to a property. Even after twenty years the thrill hadn't gone away.

"We don't have anything in," François announced. "Remember when you said you couldn't possibly stop?"

"I saw a shop or two when we came in. I'm sure we can find something there."

They set off down the drive towards the small village of Napthwaite. Arriving at the green, Darryl marvelled at the Englishness of it all. A pub on one side and a big church on the other. Charming little cottages lined the road that led them to the main drag. "It's gorgeous," he said.

"It's dead," François exclaimed.

"Everyone will be at work. It's Monday, remember," Darryl said. He would not let the cynical Frenchman ruin today.

They walked up to Queen Street. To call it a shopping place was a bit generous. This was hardly Bond Street. It had a post office, newsagents, outdoor pursuits shop, butchers and convenience store. "See? I told you it had everything we need."

The sign announcing *Poole's. Stocking everything since 2005* backed him up. They went through the door, and he almost let out a guffaw when François' face dropped.

"What the actual fuck?" he muttered.

Darryl had to feel sorry for him. François was the worst food snob he had ever met and insisted on finding the best outlets wherever in the world they were. It worked in his favour. Darryl didn't have the patience to spend hours on the internet researching places. He left that to his assistant who would then present him with a fact file, and Darryl would tweak that.

The rows of tinned meat, packet sauces and instant coffee belonged in François' worst nightmares.

"Oh, come on," Darryl said, knowing a cheery disposition would wind François up more. "I'm sure we can find a frozen pizza or something."

"A frozen…" François scowled at him, realising he was the butt of the joke. "I am prepared to buy coffee, milk and bread from this…cowshed."

"How about I buy you lunch at the pub? We can make a plan from there."

"Very well."

They were about to leave when they noticed a woman behind the counter staring at them. Short and of indiscriminate age, she watched their every move. François took an involuntary step back into Darryl, which made him want to laugh all the more.

"Nothing to your liking then?" she asked.

Her face seemed to have scowled so much it was its permanent state.

"We forgot our list," Darryl said.

Liz's scowl intensified. Darryl pushed François towards the door.

"You new round here?" she said.

"That's right." François sniffed. "Mr Burlington has bought Thorpe Hall."

She stood up a little straighter and smoothed down her tabard. "Liz Poole, Mrs," she said. "Leading local businesswoman."

Darryl stepped forward and shook her hand. "Darryl Burlington. Very pleased to meet you."

She had a look that could strip paint. Darryl had dealt with many difficult sellers and vicious executives, but women like Liz were a different breed.

"What are your plans for that place, then?" she asked, leaning forward.

"Well, we plan to—" François started but stopped when Darryl stood on his foot.

"Oh, it's early days yet, Mrs Poole. We only got here today. I want to get a feel for the place first. Find out what makes Napthwaite tick."

Her face brightened. "I can help you there. Nothing goes on round here without my knowledge."

Darryl could well believe it. He would bet that she had all the gossip, which was why he had no intention of letting her see his hand just yet. Locals didn't always warm to Burlington Hotels. "We've got a couple of months to finalise plans, so we'll be staying here. I will be sure to call in on you, or perhaps you could come to the Hall for tea?"

"That would be lovely."

"I'll say good day then."

She nodded, but her eyes never left them as they retreated onto the street.

"Staying here for the next few months? When did that idea pop into your head?" François moaned as they wandered towards the green.

"Just then but think about it. The last thing we want is a revolt, and this doesn't strike me as a place where change is all that welcome. Let's charm them for a bit first. We don't have any trips scheduled, do we?"

François sighed. "No, I was thinking about a trip to Mexico. Remember Carlos? He's never stopped emailing I fancy a bit of relaxation. You know, before Kenya."

"Frankie, can't you do that in the summer once it's all under way? You could go straight from Kefalonia. For me?"

"I suppose. And stop calling me Frankie."

Darryl put his arm around François. "I think living the village life for a bit will be fun. Who knows what trouble we can get ourselves into?"

* * * *

"*Merde.*"

Darryl poked his head around the study door. "What is the matter with you?"

François' butt stuck out from under a desk as he tried to sort out a tangle of cables. After a very enjoyable meal at the pub the day before, they had come home to a van full of furniture and equipment. François had assumed command, and they now had a very passable headquarters.

"When they were packing up our stuff, I bloody told them to remove each wire separately." He held up a mass. "Does this look separate to you?"

"No, François," Darryl said.

"You're taking the piss?"

"Yes, François."

The other man scowled and resumed his work. "You may think it's funny now, but if your stupid computer isn't working for the board meeting tomorrow, it will be my fault."

Darryl came in and sat down opposite François, holding out his hand. "Here, give me one end."

They both set to work untangling things.

"Once we've done this, I'll go to the town the landlord told us about. We need some proper food to eat," Darryl said.

Years of practice told him he could only push François so far before he became a royal pain in the arse.

"No can do," François said. "We have the old gardener coming any minute."

Darryl made a face. "Can't you handle that? I don't want to have to tell some pensioner we're putting a car park over his begonias."

"And I love doing that?"

"You're cold-blooded. You don't care," Darryl teased.

François huffed and brushed his light brown curls from his eyes. "I will do it on the condition you get me some decent wine, proper cheese and filter coffee."

"It'll be like Christmas Day all over again."

François dropped the wires. "We only drank champagne and fucked on Christmas Day."

Luckily the doorbell rang. Darryl sprang up. "If that's the gardener, I'll send him in. If you think of anything else you need, WhatsApp me."

With his assistant's mutterings echoing in his ears, Darryl grabbed his coat and keys from the hall. He hoped François would treat the old codger with kindness and remembered his lecture about not alienating the village.

The person standing on the doorstep took his breath away. He had never seen a more handsome man, and Darryl had made it his life's mission to inspect decent-looking men. "Uh…hello? Can I help you?" he stammered.

The man thrust his hand out. "Michael Fleming. Pleased to meet you."

Darryl took his hand. The strength in those calloused hands sent a chill up his spine. "Pleased to meet you too. Sorry, I'm confused."

"I'm the gardener. Didn't your assistant tell you I was calling in?"

He tried to get some sense into his head, but it seemed the blood had all rushed a little lower. "Ah yes, sorry. Darryl Burlington. Come in. We're all at sixes and sevens." He ushered the man inside.

"Were you on your way out? I can come again later, or if Mr Vernier is in, I can always speak to him."

Darryl took his coat off and flung it on the hook. He held his hand out for Michael's coat. "No trouble at all. I'm very hands-on. You can deal with me."

Michael shrugged his waxed jacket off and handed it to Darryl, who placed it on top of his.

"Come through to the kitchen. I haven't been to the shops yet, so I can only offer you tea. The previous owners left it. Is that okay?"

Michael waved him away. "No problem. I can't really stop. Gosh, it seems strange to see other things in here."

The door opened and François came in. He scowled when he saw Darryl with someone. "I thought you'd gone to the shops," he said. He walked around to face Michael and took a step back. "Hello," he said, his eyes widening.

Michael smiled. "You must be Mr Vernier. I said to Mr Burlington that we could chat about things, but he wanted to deal with it personally."

"I'm sure he did," François said, glancing at Darryl with a haughty expression. "He's very involved."

They all hopped up on the stools surrounding the island.

"I wondered if you'd had any thoughts about the garden," Michael began.

"Bad news, I'm afraid," François said.

"Yes, bad news. We've not even given it a moment's thought," Darryl interjected.

François shot him a withering glare which he pointedly ignored.

Michael visibly relaxed. "There's plenty of time. I figured you'd be doing work on this place, but there's no need for us to firm anything up until the spring. That's if you want me to continue working here?"

"Well…" François said.

"Of course," Darryl said, interrupting again. "We don't know anything about outside space. Obviously, we have a gardens department, but they are far more used to dealing with dry places. No, I think having an expert on the team, even in the short term, will be a wise move."

Michael beamed, which made Darryl's cock twitch like an antenna.

"Mr Johnstone, the previous owner, did agree to pay me a retainer through the winter. I know it's a bit soon to start talking about things like this, but I wondered…"

"Not a problem," Darryl said with his winning smile. "Just send François here an invoice and we can get that sorted out."

"That's such a relief. I hate talking money, but I thought it best to get it out of the way."

"Very wise," François said drily.

Michael hopped off the stool. "I had better let you get back to work. You've a lot to do, so I should leave you be. I'll show myself out."

As he made his exit, Darryl's eyes were drawn to the incredibly firm arse that filled Michael's cargo trousers perfectly. It would be worth rethinking the plans if he could gaze at that all day. "Nice to meet you," he called after him.

François stared at him. When they heard the door go, François also leapt off the stool. "You're keeping him on the books so you can fuck him?"

"I thought *we* could fuck him," Darryl said, rubbing his hands with glee. "Maybe our wings won't be clipped round here after all."

Chapter Four

"And it's named after the Hall?" Darryl asked.

Michael tried to see Thorpe Tarn through newcomers' eyes. It looked cold and dark on the icy January day. "Yes. Believe it or not, it's man-made. They needed a water source for the livestock so diverted some streams and now we have Thorpe Tarn."

"Bloody hell. You'd never know," Darryl said in wonder. "François, have you seen this?"

François sat on an old log, fiddling with his phone. He couldn't have been less interested. "Yes. Wonderful," he replied.

"He's more of a townie. Spending time up here is his idea of hell."

"I get the impression that's part of the appeal for you." Michael had been thinking that since his first meeting with the hotelier a week ago.

A cheeky grin appeared on Darryl's face. "Whatever gave you that idea?"

François came over to them. "I can't get a reception. I'm going back."

"Can't you deal with whatever it is later?" Darryl asked, a hint of annoyance in his voice.

François frowned, obviously picking this up too. "No, because today is the auction that you insisted we attend remotely. So, if you want that antique wardrobe and three paintings, you'd better let François work his magic."

Darryl seemed lost in thought for a second. "I do want that wardrobe. Go. I'm sure Michael won't mind babysitting me for a bit."

The idea of spending time alone with this gorgeous man was no hardship, but Michael would have to have his wits about him. On doing further internet research, he had discovered Darryl Burlington was one of the biggest players on the London gay scene. One person had tweeted that his bedpost had that many notches it had been whittled down to a toothpick.

François glanced at Michael snootily before heading along the path they had just walked down.

"I don't think he likes me very much," Michael said. He hadn't really expected to voice it but sometimes his thoughts did spill out. His mother had lectured him on trying to find a filter, but it wasn't him.

"Don't worry about it," Darryl said, seemingly unconcerned. "François comes across as the stereotypical haughty Frenchman. We all have acts we hide in. Behind there is a very caring and competent young man."

They walked along the shore of the tarn, their feet crunching on the pebbles.

"How long has he worked for you?" Michael asked.

"Coming up nine years," Darryl answered. "We've been through a lot together. I wouldn't be without him. But please don't tell him that."

They walked in silence for a minute or two. Michael thought it might be uncomfortable, but it felt like the most natural thing in the world. "Shall we cut up through the woods?" he suggested. "We come out behind the pub."

"Sure thing. You must have been here a long time — you know all the secrets of Napthwaite — but I don't detect a Yorkshire accent."

"Essex boy. Born and bred. I've been here just shy of a year. It's easy to find things out if you ask."

They reached the border of the woods and Michael found the path Ed, the farmer, had shown him when they had come out for a walk a few weeks previously.

"Do I detect a dig?" Darryl said when they got on an even keel.

Heat scorched Michael's face. "No, I didn't mean anything like that."

Darryl clapped his hand on his shoulder. Michael jumped at the contact.

"Relax, I'm only joking. Well, half-joking. I guess you've done some internet research on me."

How did he know that? "Well, yes I did," Michael admitted.

"That's okay. I don't blame you. I don't have the best reputation on there."

Suddenly something glinted in the side of Michael's vision, and he grabbed Darryl to make him stop. The other man started to say something when Michael put his finger to his lips and pointed.

There in the clearing stood a deer. It glanced around but hadn't spotted them behind the trees. Seemingly unconcerned, it continued its search for green shoots in the frozen ground.

Michael and Darryl stood rigid watching it. Michael held on to Darryl. The smell of his oaky aftershave filled Michael's nostrils. Hardly daring to breath, Michael glanced at Darryl, who seemed transfixed. It came to an end when the deer got spooked by something and silently bounded deeper into the woods.

"Fucking hell," Darryl said. "That was amazing."

Continuing up the path, they crossed right where the deer had been grazing only seconds before.

"It's a long way from Southend seafront," Michael said. "That's why I am so relieved that you're going to keep the gardens on. I'd probably have to leave, and I like it here."

"You know I'm answerable to a board. Not everything is my decision, more's the pity."

Michael snapped to attention. "Oh, sorry, I didn't realise." Everything in him wanted to ask further but he didn't want to ruin the moment. He opted to wait and see what happened.

They made it to where the path met the road and cut towards the green.

"The food at the pub was a surprise. I expected scampi and chips, but it could be London standards."

"Ah. That's my friend, Will. He used to be a chef in London but settled here last year."

"That's quite the leap of faith."

"Not really. He's from here and his father has been quite poorly. That's who you bought the Hall from."

"I remember them saying the old lad wanted to scale down. He still lives in the village though, doesn't he?"

"Certainly does. Next door to me. They own both houses. They've been good enough to let me live there rent-free until I know what is happening."

Darryl stopped. "I'm sorry that everything is up in the air for you at the moment."

"Not to worry," Michael said. He didn't want Darryl to think the only reason he had asked him on a walk was to interrogate him. "I'm sure when you know what you have planned for the Hall, you will let me know."

"Of course," Darryl said.

They resumed walking up to the shops.

"I need to call into the newsagents," Darryl said. "François is on at me to get a paper delivered. He hates reading it on the tablet. God knows why — he spends the rest of the day glued to that bloody thing."

François intimidated Michael a little. It had been a long time since he had met someone quite so openly hostile. He wondered what the dynamic was below the surface.

They went into Brockbank's shop. Kathleen was refilling the shelves with greeting cards that no one would ever buy through choice. She did a roaring trade on forgotten birthdays so never made any effort to get any decent stock in.

"Hello, Michael," she said, straightening up. "Who do we have here?"

"Darryl Burlington. Pleased to meet you."

"Kathleen Brockbank. Yes, I've heard about you. You've bought the Hall." She stalked to her cash register before turning around.

"Word travels fast round here," Darryl said with a laugh. He selected a *Financial Times* and *Independent* then took them to the counter.

Kathleen rang them up on the ancient till.

"Hang on," Darryl said. He darted to the newspaper stand and picked up a local paper. "Never hurts to know what's going on under your nose too."

Kathleen raised an eyebrow to Michael. "If you want to know that, you need to ask the right people."

Darryl gave her a smile. "I suppose you would be one of those people."

"We're a close-knit village, Mr Burlington. We all know what is going on or at least it doesn't take us long to find out. That'll be six-fifty, please."

Darryl handed her a ten-pound note.

"Put the change in the Mountain Rescue tin," he said, gesturing to the charity collection jar on the counter.

"Very generous," Kathleen said. Her face suggested she found him anything but.

Michael had no doubt that Darryl would have dealt with much tougher people than Kathleen Brockbank. Even so, she had no excuse for being that rude.

They went out onto the street.

"They're not naturally friendly round here, are they? I got the same from the woman in the shop over the road."

"I wouldn't take it personally," Michael said. They strolled towards the green. "The Hall hasn't been sold for hundreds of years. It's a big deal. Whatever happens will have a massive impact on the village."

"No pressure on me then," Darryl mused. "Change can be a good thing for a place like this too, you know."

"I know. It's not me you'll have to convince though."

They walked in silence for a while until they reached the gates of the Hall.

"Do you want to come up for a drink?" Darryl offered.

"I'd better not. I spend the winter months researching. I'm thinking of writing a book at some point."

Darryl's face lit up. "A book? That's impressive."

"It might be, if I ever do it," Michael said, looking away. "I'll be seeing you."

"Michael?" Darryl called after him.

He turned.

"Do you fancy coming for dinner tomorrow night? François might be a royal pain in the arse sometimes, but he's a brilliant cook."

Michael laughed. "I'd love to."

"Good. It's a date then."

* * * *

Michael threw himself into researching his book on designing fun zones for gardens. He'd been inspired to write it following the work he'd done with Matthew at the Hall. After a day hard at work, Michael liked the idea of going to the Hall for dinner. It would take some time to get used to visiting new people up there, but he liked Darryl. The jury was out on François.

As he tried on different shirts, there was a knock at the door. He opened it to find Will on the step.

"Hello. Wow, very sharp," he said. "I had come to see if you fancied coming to Holton to the movies, but I suspect you've had a better offer."

Michael showed him in. "Not really. I've been invited up to the Hall for dinner."

Will slumped down in the sofa and glanced at his watch. "It's four o'clock. They eat early up there."

Michael sat opposite him. "I'm not there until seven. I thought I'd get a head start in what I'm wearing. I've been so used to just putting on a T-shirt and a fleece, so I'm out of practice."

Will raised an eyebrow. "I'm flying solo tonight then." He sighed. "Two lovers and no date. Story of my life."

"What are they up to tonight?"

"Andrew is at a parish council meeting and Hardeep is staying with Satinder. She's still reeling from losing Mohinder. They were close."

Michael hadn't had much to do with Hardeep's mother, but he remembered a force to be reckoned with, standing behind the counter at the post office. "Such a shame she didn't make it back from India to see him happy."

Will seemed distracted. "Yeah, but she was also one of the last reasons for us to stay a secret. Who knows eh? Anyway, let's talk about you. Which one are you after? The boss or the boy?"

Michael flinched. Will's directness often came as a shock. "Neither, thank you. I want them to carry on paying me. Nothing more." Did he really believe that? Will's face told him he certainly didn't.

"Sure. I suppose I'd better leave you to your three-hour getting ready ritual." He got up and walked over to the door. "For an event you're not that bothered about." With a cheeky wave, he left.

He had been rumbled. He hoped he wasn't this obvious to everyone else.

* * * *

Four hours later and the intensity of the scowl from François across the dining table confirmed that maybe he had been a little obvious.

Regardless of his feelings about their guest, François had laid on an amazing meal of Beef Bourguignon with all the trimmings.

"This is wonderful. Thank you," Michael said, digging in. He missed big meals. Living on his own, he often made do with a ready meal from Poole's shop.

François nodded in acceptance of the compliment. Darryl looked dangerously sexy in a crisp white shirt that fitted like a second skin. François had on a tight blue T-shirt that showed off a body an athlete would be proud of.

Michael thanked his lucky stars he had made the effort with a slim-fitting denim shirt. An old T-shirt wouldn't have made the grade.

"François, why don't you ask Michael for help with your little problem?"

Michael looked to François.

"We seem to have squirrels in the green bedroom," François said. "I was measuring up in there today and one of the little *conards* sat on the bookshelf. As bold as brass."

"Not again," Michael said. "They were here last winter when I arrived. They get in from the old oak tree. I told Matthew the branches were too close to the house, but he wouldn't hear of me trimming it. Something about an ancestor of his having a tree house in there."

Darryl took a sip of his wine. "I knew there would be a reason. What can we do?"

He thought about this for a second. "They don't like vinegar. I would recommend soaking a load of rags in the stuff and filling the room."

"Can you chop the tree down? It's not like we'll be needing it," François interjected.

He thought about his conversation with Matthew. It had meant so much to him. It would upset the already frail man if they felled the tree in the first few weeks of the new people being in.

"How about I trim it?" he offered. "I can come and do it in the week."

"Sounds perfect," Darryl said.

"Always vermin," François said with a shudder. "Do you remember that place in Sao Paolo? Absolutely rat infested. I'd rather have a cute squirrel than a stinking rat."

"There's not a lot of difference," Michael said. "Squirrels are just rats with a cuter wardrobe."

Darryl guffawed loudly, but François' face showed he found this contradiction anything but amusing. "Perhaps you should come *early* in the week," he said.

Michael enjoyed making Darryl laugh and had especially liked the happy gaze that had rested on him since. "Thinking about it, I'm not sure the next few days or so would work—didn't you see the forecast? Storm Jeremy is coming. They reckon it might be a bad one too."

Darryl frowned. "I hadn't seen that. Do you get many storms here?"

"No more than anywhere else," Michael answered. "But the houses are all pretty old. It will take more than a bit of wind to damage Napthwaite."

François chuckled to himself as he speared an asparagus tip.

"Something you'd like to share with the group?" Darryl asked.

"*Moi?*" François said, mock innocence on his face.

"Yes, you," Darryl said.

Michael felt unease running up the back of his neck. He knew he shouldn't have made the squirrel gag.

"I just thought it was interesting. The whole 'we stand against change' line. You know...with what's coming." François flashed a malevolent glare at Michael.

"What does that mean?" Michael said to Darryl.

Darryl had the grace to look embarrassed. He put his knife and fork down. "You'll have to excuse François' melodramatics. What I presume he means is that this place won't be a private home. It will be a commercial property. That's going to have an effect on Napthwaite. I like to think for the good."

With the bare truth out, Michael felt winded. The change of use for Thorpe Hall would have a huge impact, it was true. It just felt cold discussing it in what he still felt was Matthew's dining room. "Tell me about your trip to Greece," he said, desperate to change the conversation. "I've never been."

Darryl started regaling him with stories of a property they had bought. But Michael's glance went from Darryl to François and back again. He couldn't deny he felt drawn to them, but the impact they were going to have on the lives of people he had grown to care about made him worried.

"To cut a long story short, I told the guy I would donate to the local donkey sanctuary and he cut us a deal. François, did we do that donation?"

François nodded. "I went for the 'name a donkey' option."

"What?" Darryl asked, amused.

"*Oui.* Darryl the donkey is having a high old life, thanks to you."

They burst into laughter. But the joke was lost on Michael.

They don't even care what damage they do.

Chapter Five

The winds were picking up as Michael fought his way down Queen Street.

"It took its sweet time, but this storm is going to give us a battering today," Christine Carrington said to him as he made his way into Poole's.

"Is everything all right with you?" he asked.

"We've closed the school. Better to be safe than sorry. The kids were annoyed old Storm Jeremy waited until Friday to show up, of course."

Christine was the head teacher at the local primary school, and she had a point. After his meal at the Hall last Sunday, Michael had been watching the weather forecast avidly. One because he hated storms and two, he quite fancied an excuse to go up there to trim that tree.

He made his way to the back of the shop. The meal that François had prepared had inspired him to get his recipe books out. So far this week he had burnt a risotto and undercooked a chicken breast that had meant a night of running to the loo.

Eventually Will had taken pity on him and given him some beginner recipes. Tonight, he would attempt a cottage pie. The butchers had been shut up when he got there and of course, Poole's only had frozen mince which both Will and François would probably shudder at, but needs must.

He had set himself up with a supermarket order the next week but slots went quickly in these parts so he would have to make do until then.

Once he'd got all the ingredients needed, he went up to the counter. Thankfully it was Liz's son serving.

"Afternoon, Dean. How are you today?"

"All good, thank you. I bet there'll be some work for you after tonight."

"Work?"

"With the storm. Plenty of things needing clearing. What does a gardener do in the winter?"

The number of times he'd been asked that… "There's still plenty to do getting it ready." He made a mental note to speak to Darryl about getting access to the grounds.

"Ah yes. Planning. I understand," Dean said, tapping his nose.

"We also drink copious amounts of wine and hatch plans for storms. Didn't you know?"

"I suspected it, but thanks for the confirmation."

After paying, Michael made his way home. He didn't want to be out in the horrible weather much longer. Before he went into the house, he knocked on Mrs Turnbull's door. She lived on the other side of him, and he worried about her. "Hello, Mrs T. Everything all right? You all secure for tonight?"

"I'm fine, thank you, son," she said, smiling. "You're a good lad for checking."

"If you need anything, just holler. I'm a light sleeper."

"I will do that. Hang on a minute." She disappeared into the house and came out with a plastic box. "There's some meat and potato pie in there. Fresh out of the oven. It will go lovely with some mash and veggies."

Mrs Turnbull regularly forced her freshly baked cakes and biscuits on him and as he had never tasted better, he never refused.

"You spoil me, Mrs T."

"That's because you deserve it. Now go on with you."

She closed the door, and he went into his house. The mince could go straight into his freezer. There was no point in looking a gift horse in the mouth. Just as he set about peeling potatoes, there was a knock at the door. He quickly opened it to find Matthew standing on the step. The speed of Matthew's decline made Michael sad, but Matthew seemed happy. What an unfair trade-off.

"Hello, Matthew. Come in."

"I won't, if it's all the same. I popped round to see if you had any candles. No doubt the bloody power will go off at the first sign of this confounded storm."

"Of course. Come in for a second out of that wind."

Matthew tottered in while Michael rooted around in the kitchen cupboards. He found a box and pulled out half a dozen.

"I knew I had them. I'm surprised you're not prepared," he said, handing them over.

"We're still all over the place in there. Most of our stuff is in storage."

Michael hadn't had much time to speak to Matthew since the sale of the Hall. "Are you happy in there?"

"It's still the honeymoon period. We're both being very nice to each other. I wonder what will happen when that wears off."

Michael thought about the tension between Will and Matthew when Will had first come back to Napthwaite. To have that in a small cottage wouldn't be fun for either of them. He made a mental note to do more things with Will. He might have Andrew and Hardeep plus his work at the pub, but sometimes a friend was needed above everything else.

"Can I help you home?"

"Don't be ridiculous. I've been walking these streets for nearly eighty years." Matthew shuffled to the door before stopping. "Is everything all right up there?"

By keeping ties with the Hall, Michael had a suspicion he would be stuck in the middle between the old and new guard. It could get uncomfortable. "As far as I can tell."

"No talk of what they have planned?"

"Nothing yet. I'm just grateful to still be on the payroll."

Matthew's face softened. "I'm sorry."

Michael instantly regretted his comment. "It's fine. I understand you had to sell the place."

"You're a good man, Michael."

Matthew left the house, gently closing the door after him. For the rest of the evening, Michael battled guilt pangs for saying what he had. He resolved to make amends the following day by offering to take Matthew for dinner at The King's. It would be nice for them to eat some of Will's food.

He went to bed. Outside, the wind whipped through the trees that lined the street. They could do with a trim too. He snuggled under the duvet. Stormy nights made him feel cosy in bed. They always had.

Three hours later, Michael awoke with a start. A terrible groaning noise cut through the night's silence. It was coming from outside. Bleary-eyed and disorientated, he dragged himself out of bed. As he drew the curtains back, he heard a scream. An agitated Mrs Turnbull stood on the street, looking at one of the trees right outside the window. It swayed in a terrible fashion. The roots were lifting the grass up.

Quick as a flash, he pulled on his jogging trousers and a hoodie. As he dashed down the stairs, there was a sickening crack, and everything went black.

He came to with hands on his body.

"Michael?"

It was his neighbour, David Chan.

"What happened?" he said.

"Can you move?"

Mentally he checked his body. He had no pain except in his side where he'd hit the banister as he'd fallen down the stairs.

Everything was dark except for the flashlight someone pointed at him.

"We need to get you out of here," David said.

He helped Michael get to his feet and they staggered to the porch. Still not understanding what had happened, he shoved his feet into his walking boots and went onto the street.

A small crowd had gathered. Mrs Turnbull ran over to him.

"Our houses."

To his horror he saw that the tree had smashed into the three cottages. The old roof that lined all three had been no match for the heavy tree and it had gone straight into the bedrooms. If he'd stayed in bed, he would have been killed.

"Jesus Christ," he said, shocked.

"Dad!"

Will Johnstone came dashing over the green. He tried to push his way through the crowd to get into the house, but Michael grabbed him.

"Will, you can't. It's unsafe. Has anyone called the fire brigade?"

"Everything is down. The power and the phone lines."

Michael remembered that Matthew had had a generator installed in the Hall. "Keep hold of him," he said to David. Taking a second to tie his laces, he ran down the road towards the Hall. He didn't feel the cold or out of breath as he dashed up the drive to the big door. Banging on it for all he was worth, he almost cried with joy when a light came on.

"Darryl. François."

Another light, and at last he heard voices. A dishevelled François greeted him.

"What do you want?"

"Michael?" Darryl said behind him.

"I'm sorry to wake you but a tree's come down on the green. It smashed through my house and others. I don't know if everyone's out, but the power is down."

Darryl kicked into action. "François, use the internet phone. It should be working—I paid enough for that connection. Come in. Give me a second to get dressed."

Darryl ran up the stairs three at a time. Standing in the hall, Michael started to shake. He wasn't sure if it was the cold or shock.

When Darryl returned in jeans and a jumper, he saw Michael shivering in just his hoodie. "Here," he said, handing him a duck-down jacket. "Do you want to borrow some warmer clothes too?"

"I need to get back."

"Of course, you do. François, follow us down as soon as you get through. Is there a connection?"

"I'm on to them now," François shouted from the room.

"Thank fuck for cable, eh?" Darryl said grimly.

They got to the crowd outside the cottages in record time.

"Fuck me," Darryl exclaimed when he saw the huge tree that had caved in the three houses.

"Where's Will?" Michael said, scanning the party.

David shook his head. Michael saw the open door to the Johnstones' cottage and made his way toward it.

Darryl took hold of his arm. "Don't even think about it."

But Michael owed the Johnstones a lot, and he wouldn't let Will go through this alone. He pulled away from Darryl and ran into the house.

Twigs and branches had even fallen through into the living room. A bough cut across the stairs, but Michael clambered over it. The steps gave an ominous creak, but he wouldn't be stopped. Getting his footing, he managed to make his way to the top. Guessing that Matthew had the front bedroom, he went in.

The damage looked bad. The main body of the tree had smashed through the window. To his horror, illuminated by moonlight, he saw the bodies of Matthew Johnstone and his beloved alsatian, Titus, half underneath...lying perfectly still in the bed.

Will crouched against the wall, totally still. Crawling under a branch to get to the bed, Michael grabbed

Matthew's outstretched hand. He clutched the wrist, curling his fingers tightly, desperate to find a pulse.

"Don't bother," Will said, quietly. "He's gone."

"But—" Michael swallowed. There was no sign of life. His hand shaking, he gently replaced the elderly man's wrist on the fur of his faithful friend then fought his way to Will. Slumping down on the floor, he drew him close. Maybe his touch brought Will out of his trance, but sobs that seemed to come from his feet broke out.

"Oh God, Dad," he cried at the top of his lungs. Michael held him as tightly as possible and let his own tears fall.

They sat like that for what seemed like hours but could only have been about ten minutes. Blue lights lit up the dark night. The sound of machinery and shouts cut through the silence.

"They're coming now, Will. We should go."

"I can't."

"It's all right. They'll look after them." Michael got up and held his hand out to Will.

"You promise?"

He nodded.

Will allowed himself to be led out of the room. A fireman waited for them at the bottom of the stairs.

"Are you injured?" he called up.

"No, we're fine."

Michael let Will go first, and he managed to get over the branch. Michael followed. Once Will had got safely out of the house, he took hold of the fireman's arm. "There's a fatality."

The fireman nodded. There was nothing else to say. Michael went out to the crowd. By now Andrew and

Hardeep had arrived and were trying to comfort a sobbing Will.

Mrs Turnbull ran up to him. "But what's happened to Matthew? Will they get him out?" Her tear-stained face was etched with worry. She might be the town busybody, but Michael had grown to care for her.

"Mrs Turnbull, I'm so sorry. Matthew's gone."

Darryl leapt forward in the nick of time and grabbed hold as her legs gave way. "Oh no. Not Matthew," she cried out.

Michael helped Darryl to move her out of the way of the further emergency services that were arriving. He had never seen the green so busy.

"We'll be opening The King's for anyone who needs it," James announced. "We've no electric or gas but we've got beds."

Darryl stepped forward. "We have power at the Hall and six bedrooms. Everyone must come to us. I insist."

"Are you sure?" James asked.

"Of course. We don't have much in to feed anyone."

"I can fix that," James said.

He, Ed and Arthur dashed to The King's. Michael, still holding a sobbing Mrs Turnbull, looked at Darryl. "That's very kind of you."

"Do you expect me to share my room?" François asked.

Darryl whirled around on him. For a second, Michael thought he was going to hit him.

"That room happens to be *my* room, like all the others. You won't be sharing it. You'll be surrendering it. You can sleep in the study on the sofa."

"But—"

"End of discussion."

François sighed dramatically. "Fine. Have it your bloody way."

After an hour or two of dealing with emergency services and securing their homes as best they could, the villagers made a bizarre procession up to the big house.

Once Matthew's body had been brought out of the cottage, Will went to Andrew's, where Hardeep and Satinder had joined them. It took hours before they settled Mrs Turnbull, the Chans, the Holdsworths, the Burtons and the three guys from The King's Arms pub into their respective rooms in the Hall.

Michael and Darryl stood in the kitchen, taking big sips from the brandies François had poured for them.

"I wonder how long ago the Hall had this many people in it," Darryl mused.

"Decades," Michael said.

The clock gently struck four times.

"We should get to bed," Darryl said. "I have a Zoom call with the bloody board at ten. I will look like shit. They're already moaning about us not getting on with this place. God knows what they'll think if they find out half the village are sleeping here for free."

François had already gone into the study. Maybe Michael had misjudged him earlier on. Once they had arrived at the Hall, he had been a marvel. He'd sorted drinks, food and lodgings for everyone.

"Where am I sleeping?" Michael said, the fatigue overcoming him.

"Only one bed left," Darryl said. "Mine. Come on."

Michael tensed up. Surely this man didn't expect anything after the night they'd had?

Darryl stopped at the door and must have sensed his hesitation. "Give me some credit," he said, shaking his head.

Ashamed, Michael followed him. The shame was twofold. Firstly that he'd misjudged him and secondly, after everything that had happened, he so desperately wanted to get into bed with this man.

Chapter Six

Darryl lay in the bed, hardly daring to move. Michael had his back to him and snored gently. He thought about the night's events. A man dead and houses destroyed.

There was movement on the landing outside and voices in the kitchen below. The villagers must be getting up.

Slowly he moved his head to look at the clock.

Eight o'clock.

"I'm awake," Michael said, making Darryl jump.

Finally able to move freely, he sat up against the pillow. Michael did the same and glanced across at him. Darryl tried his best not to stare at Michael's muscular hairy chest exposed by the duvet dropping down tantalisingly close to his waist.

"How are you feeling?"

Michael shook his head. "I can't believe it. Poor Will. What he must be feeling today."

In the distance downstairs, François could be heard ushering people through to the dining room. He drove

Darryl mad sometimes, but he had shown his worth last night.

"I should go down," Michael said, making to get out of bed.

Darryl grabbed hold of his arm. "Don't worry if you don't feel like it. Our French friend has everyone under control."

Michael allowed Darryl to guide him back to the pillow. "I can't really face them, if I'm honest. Seeing him under that tree and Titus too. It's too much."

He collapsed into floods of tears. Darryl snaked his arm around his shoulders and hugged him. Michael's tears fell onto his bare chest. His body curled up around Darryl's side, and his arm held on to his chest for dear life.

Do not get a hard-on, Burlington. For fuck's sake.

To hear the raw pain falling out of this man was anything but sexy. Darryl just held him and let the emotion cascade out. Eventually just a few wracking sobs remained.

"I'm sorry," Michael said, sitting up. "I snotted on your chest."

Putting on his best brave face, Darryl reached for the box of tissues by the bed. Quickly, but without appearing too urgent, he wiped his chest and handed the rest to Michael.

"Better?" Darryl asked.

"Better." Michael nodded. "This time I am going to get up. I need to see everyone. I'll walk down with them and see the damage at home. Thank you for letting me stay."

He climbed out of the bed. Darryl did allow himself to check out the handsome man before him. He'd known he would have an incredible body, and Michael didn't disappoint. His muscular frame was lightly dusted with dark brown hair, leading down to an eye-watering package framed in white Calvin Klein briefs.

Darryl's cock gave up the fight and sprang to attention. He had no chance of controlling it.

"Getting a good view?" Michael asked, pulling on his jogging trousers.

"Hey, I'm only human." Darryl smiled, putting his hands behind his head.

Michael pulled a T-shirt on. "I dread to think what state my house is in. It's been raining all night. I'll be lucky if I have the clothes I'm wearing."

His cock deciding to retreat, Darryl hopped out of bed and walked across the room to get his robe. A small stab of victory played through him when Michael stopped lacing his trainers and watched him. He would let that one slide. *For now.*

"I want you to salvage what you can and when you're ready, come back up here. You'll stay with us for as long as it takes," Darryl said.

Michael stood up. "I can't let you do that. You don't really want me here. You're just saying it to be nice."

Darryl put his hands on both Michael's shoulders. "Michael Fleming. I am a Black man from the wrong side of the tracks who has been on the *Sunday Times* Rich List for the last eight years. I did not achieve this feat by doing things I don't want to do or saying things just to be nice."

Michael laughed. Darryl noticed his eyes crinkled up at the side. He liked it.

"Thank you, but honestly…"

"I also get what I want ninety-nine percent of the time. The one percent I ignore, because otherwise I'd be spoilt." He gripped Michael's shoulders. "You can even have your own room tonight."

"Okay, you win. Thank you."

"Of course, if you wanted to bunk in with me again, I wouldn't put up much of a fight," Darryl said, slyly.

Michael blushed. "Let me get through the day first before we worry about the night."

Darryl took his hands off Michael's shoulders, and Michael walked to the door. He stopped. "Thank you again, Darryl, and I don't believe you when you say you don't do nice things."

Before Darryl could formulate a suitably witty response, Michael had slunk out of the room. Darryl stared at the closed door for a second or two.

Shit. I like him.

* * * *

The rest of the day passed without incident. Once he'd discussed the progress of Thorpe Hall with the board, François had a huge list of things for them to go through. *Who would have thought choosing bed linen could be so involved?*

Darryl kept glancing at the clock on the mantel. Michael had been gone hours. To Darryl's bemusement he had butterflies at the thought of him returning.

"Did I tell you Michael is staying with us for a while?" he said.

François was comparing two practically identical fleur de lis patterns. "I guessed you'd take pity on him. I presume you won't be giving him my bedroom."

Darryl ruffled François' hair. "You were great last night, Frankie."

François blushed and adjusted his fringe. "I have changed my bed. Mrs Turnbull doesn't strike me as the cleanest."

"You don't fool me, François Vernier. You were worried about them all last night."

"It was a terrible thing that happened. Was Michael all right when he left? I didn't get a chance to speak to him."

Darryl exhaled. "He's devastated. I think he and the old guy must have got close when he worked for him."

François studied him for a second. "You like him, don't you?"

"Yes, he's a nice guy."

"It's more than that."

"He's a sexy nice guy. Don't you think?"

His assistant nodded. "Very sexy indeed. A bit of a Goody Two-Shoes, though. If you're planning anything, I wouldn't hold your breath. As sexy as you are, even some men are immune to the Burlington charm."

"Either way, it won't hurt to have him around the place, will it?"

"I'll go and change the purple room. You can look on that machine for some help. I'm not playing housekeeper forever."

"I'll cancel the French maid's outfit then," Darryl shouted after him.

Michael returned to the house about half an hour after that. François showed him up to his room and they left him to it for a while. He'd seemed exhausted.

Powering down the laptop, Darryl went in search of François. There were some decent smells coming from the kitchen.

"What's cooking, good-looking?" Darryl said.

"Just a chicken casserole," François replied.

Darryl marvelled at how François varied depending on the setting. At work he was snippy, in the kitchen he was calm and in bed he was wild. Darryl quite liked it.

"Smells amazing," Darryl said, going to the fridge to get a bottle of wine out.

"*Merci.*"

Darryl searched for a corkscrew. François watched him struggle for a minute. "Oh, for goodness' sake." He laughed. "The drawer over there. Do I need to give you a tour of your own kitchen again?"

Darryl followed where he was pointing and found the item in question.

"I don't know what you would do without me," François muttered.

"Hopefully I'll never find out," Darryl said, walking up behind him and goosing him.

François jumped. "I nearly spilt that then. What's got into you? I haven't seen you like this since Greece."

Darryl winked. "Maybe I'm in the same mood as Greece."

"I'm always in the same mood as Greece," François muttered.

François would have sex morning, noon and night if Darryl let him. That wasn't to say Darryl didn't have urges, but they had a rule. They only played with others. Things would get terribly complicated if they ever broke that. He valued François too much, both personally and professionally, to risk losing it.

A bleary-eyed Michael came into the kitchen, breaking the spell.

"Hi. You must have heard the wine bottle opening," Darryl said.

Michael smiled. "I smelt something amazing."

François reddened. The way into his heart and his pants was to compliment his cooking. Darryl poured them all glasses and handed one to Michael.

"Get that into you. You deserve it." A toast felt inappropriate, so Darryl hastily took a swig of his glass.

"I can't thank you both enough. The house is a total mess."

"As long as it takes, you have a bed here," Darryl said.

"Then I'll definitely get that branch sorted out tomorrow."

François winked at Darryl. "Then I'll definitely be watching from the window."

Michael stared from one to the other before becoming overly interested in the pan that François stirred. "What's in there?"

"Mulled wine. Just because it's not Christmas doesn't mean we can't have any."

Michael took a sniff. "I hope you're not trying to get me drunk."

Darryl put a hand on his arm. "We're always trying to get drunk in this house."

They chatted for a while until François finally got the casserole out of the oven and plated up three portions. He coupled it with roasted new potatoes and warm bread.

Darryl's mouth watered but, as he watched Michael digging in, his appetite for chicken waned. He wanted a whole different kind of meat tonight.

Chapter Seven

Michael put his knife and fork down. That was the second delicious meal François had cooked for him. The man had skills. "I needed that. Thank you."

François seemed pleased at the praise. Michael couldn't work him out. One minute he protected Darryl as though his life depended on it and the next, he thoughtfully dealt with the displaced villagers.

Michael admitted to himself that François intimidated him. Darryl, on the other hand, had a different brand of self-confidence. He had made it huge in his life but didn't seem to have done that at the expense of others. Even as he'd been dealing with the wreckage of his home and the emotions of the day, Michael hadn't been able to get Darryl out of his mind.

As he'd walked up the path to the Hall, which he'd walked so many times before, he found himself excited to see him again. His mother had always told him if he was invited to share food with people, he had to earn his keep. So he hopped off the barstool and started to clear up some of the dishes.

"What are you doing?" François asked, clearly shocked.

"You must let me wash up."

"Pah," François said, waving his hand. "I will do it in the morning. You are our guest."

"But—"

"Don't try to argue with François." Darryl grinned. "I think I've won one argument in all the time I've known him."

François raised an eyebrow. "That's because your wish is usually my command, and you never have to put up a fight."

"I suppose that's true."

"How long did you say you'd been together?" Michael asked, taking a sip of his wine. It was good stuff. In fact, everything they had brought to the Hall — furniture, food, wine — seemed to be of the best quality. It would be interesting to see what other changes they brought with them. "Over eight years, right?"

François nodded. "I was in a bit of a mess. I came over to the UK with not much of a plan and things got on top of me. Darryl here gave me a chance and it's been fun, fun, fun, ever since."

The two shared a look. Michael suspected more to this story than met the eye, but he didn't like to push. "When do you think work will begin on this place?" he continued.

"I think another month yet," Darryl replied. "I've heard the snow can hit pretty hard up here. I hate projects that stop and start."

"You'll see a different side to him then. He becomes quite the sergeant major," François said with a wink.

Darryl play-swatted him. "I don't mind paying for quality, but I'm not a fool."

"Quite right."

After the events of the last twenty-four hours, Michael really enjoyed being in these two men's company. The village had been rocked, and that afternoon had been so difficult. It felt like a release to be listening to Darryl and François bantering. Guilt swirled around in his chest. He sat here enjoying a lovely meal while Will was the other side of the village going through hell.

He hadn't seen him today. Mrs Turnbull had said that he'd been down earlier to get some things. Michael vowed that he would go up there in a day or so to pay his respects.

"You okay?"

Michael snapped to the present to find Darryl looking at him. "Yeah, sorry."

"Nothing to be sorry about."

He didn't want to bring the mood down. These two were excited about their new project — they didn't want him with a long face.

"Maybe I should hit the sack," Michael said. "Leave you guys to your evening. I've invaded your lives enough."

Darryl drained his glass. "You don't have to go to bed on our account. If you're tired, fair enough."

He wasn't tired. He'd had a sleep that afternoon when he'd got back from the village. The stress of the afternoon had taken its toll. At that moment he was more awake than he'd been in a long time. "You know, I'm not. I thought I would be after not getting much sleep last night."

"You snored enough," Darryl teased.

Michael felt heat spread across his face. His ex had told him he snored, and he hated it.

"Don't tease him," François chided Darryl.

"So, three grown men not tired. What are we to do?" Darryl continued. "Only one thing for it."

Michael frowned.

"Monopoly."

François groaned. "Absolutely not. I spend my days watching you making money. That's enough for anyone."

Michael laughed, the horror on François' face tickling him.

"I guess we'll have to have sex then," Darryl said.

Michael thought he had heard wrong for a second. He glanced from one to the other, adrenalin instantly flooding his system.

"Now that I could be on board with," François said.

"What?" he managed. The two men's eyes on him were making him nervous.

"Relax. If that's not your thing, fair enough. But you must admit being thrown together after a huge storm…it's pretty sexy," Darryl said.

The way that he proposed it made Michael feel no pressure whatsoever. He could have refused and gone to his room with no more being said about it. He didn't know if the wine had made him reckless or the fact that his world had been turned upside down, but he felt so close to the two men staring at him. "I didn't realise you two were *together*."

François let out a snigger. "We're not together, together. But we have our fun."

He might not be the most confident person around, but Michael hadn't lived a sheltered life either. When he had been a student at university, he had become involved with two older men. They'd had a lot of fun together and it only ended when he took a job at the other end of the country. He still sent them a Christmas card.

His cock twitched at the thought of the two men across from him naked. He only had to say the word. "Well, I hate to sleep alone," he said.

François jumped off the stool and came round the island in record time. He ran his hand over Michael's chest. "Who the fuck mentioned sleep?" he said.

Michael took one more second to appraise the handsome Frenchman whose breath tickled his neck. Then he jumped in and pressed his lips to his.

It had been months since Michael had kissed anyone, and François' soft lips were like heaven. The kiss startled gently, but as the passion coursed through Michael's body, he wanted more. He pushed his tongue into François' mouth and was eagerly received. François reached behind his head to pull him closer.

François moved between Michael's legs on the stool and they continued kissing furiously. Michael felt as though he were sliding down a helter-skelter. His cock hardened as François pushed his body against him. The fact that Darryl was watching them made it all the more arousing.

Michael ran his hands through François' hair and down his back, resting on the waistband of his trousers. How he wanted to explore what lay below.

They came up for air and looked at Darryl.

"I think this calls for champagne," Darryl announced.

"I'll get it," François said. He detached himself from Michael and walked over to the fridge, making absolutely no attempt to hide his huge erection.

Darryl held his hand out to Michael, who hopped off his stool. Ever since he'd first seen him on the internet on Christmas night, he'd wondered what it would be like to kiss him. Now he was about to find out.

Their lips clashed and Darryl squeezed his arse cheeks. Michael let out an involuntary gasp as their tongues explored each other's mouth. Running his hand up Darryl's chest, he gripped his shoulder to steady himself. Their kiss became more intense and with his other hand, he held Darryl's.

In one way, he never wanted this to end. In another, he wanted to be naked with these two men immediately.

They broke their kiss at the sound of a cork popping. François poured three glasses and handed them each one.

"Let's take this upstairs," Darryl said.

Darryl led him by the hand upstairs with François following. Michael was relieved that Darryl had taken Will's old room. It would have been strange doing this in Matthew's, but they were using that for storage mainly.

Once inside, they began pawing at one another's clothes. Michael tugged at François' shirt which he shrugged off. His hairless, toned body was so soft to the touch. Michael ran his hands across his tan skin.

Darryl pulled his T-shirt over his head and dropped his trousers to reveal white boxers. Michael palmed his cock, making Darryl groan. François pulled at Michael's shirt and dragged it off him. He leant down and nibbled at Michael's nipple, making tingles course through his spine.

Michael almost cried out when Darryl set to work on the other one. God, he needed this.

The two men raised their heads. All three mouths came together, tongues lashing against one another. Michael's cock strained at the confines of his briefs.

As if in perfect synchronisation, they quickly removed the rest of their clothes. Darryl was muscular with deep brown skin that complemented his even darker eyes. François had olive skin. Neither of them seemed to have a hair on their bodies. For a second self-consciousness overcame Michael at his hairy chest and legs, but the other two men couldn't seem to take their hands off him.

Collapsing onto the bed, they became a tangle of limbs. François grabbed at the waistband of Michael's briefs, and, finally naked, Michael lay on top of Darryl.

Michael let out a moan as François buried his face in his arse crack, his tongue instantly finding Michael's hole. Little electric shocks ricocheted around him as François teased and worried it. Moving out of the kiss, he stared into Darryl's eyes. He was so handsome and sure of himself.

François moved up Michael's body, kissing his back and neck. His hard cock pressed against Michael.

"Suck my dick," Darryl said.

François rolled off to make way for Michael. He crawled down Darryl's body and removed his boxers. His hard cock needed attention, which Michael was only too pleased to give.

Pre-cum oozed from the tip as he leant down, licking the end clean. He glanced up. Both men were watching him eagerly. If this was an audition, he had every intention of getting the role. He teased the end with his tongue, circling faster but keeping it light. Darryl sank his head on the pillow. Just as he seemed to be getting used to this, Michael plunged his cock into his mouth, sliding his lips all the way down to the base.

"Jesus, fuck," Darryl cried out.

Michael sucked greedily. When he could take no more, he looked up. The other two were kissing furiously. Michael moved over and pawed at François' boxers, the last piece of clothing to be removed before they were all naked together.

François revealed the biggest dick Michael had ever seen in his life. For a second Michael was taken aback. But he didn't want to show it and went to work, licking the outside before taking the swollen head in his mouth.

François made a noise and pushed his hips forward, teasing Michael to take more, which he did. Darryl was no slouch in the cock department, but this was a whole other level and he had to focus not to let his gag reflex kick in.

"We are terrible hosts," François declared as Michael leant back, panting. He moved from Darryl and ran his hands over Michael, who knelt at the foot of the bed, his gentle touch sending waves of pleasure through him. François kissed him lightly on the lips, his lips made Michael lightheaded. François beckoned Michael so he lay next to Darryl.

François' tongue flicked in and out of Michael's mouth, as if testing him. Then, out of nowhere, he straddled him. Michael's cock lay in the crack of his arse as François pushed his mouth onto his.

The change in tempo took Michael by surprise, but he could match him. He dragged his fingers up François' body and into his hair. He gently tugged so François' head tilted back.

"Ah, you can play soft or hard," François murmured. "I like that."

If he wanted hard, he would get it. Michael pushed his head down and François complied. He crouched over his cock, glanced at Darryl before devouring it. Darryl sat watching the two of them, stroking his own dick.

Michael held his arm out and Darryl moved towards him, their lips meeting as François sucked hard on his dick. It felt so good to have these two men working on him.

He stroked Darryl's soft skin with one hand and nestled his other in François' hair. The two moved onto their knees, kissing above him. He grabbed both their cocks and massaged. They both ground their hips in time with him, giving him a show that made his cock harder if possible.

"Oh God, I want to feel your cum," he murmured.

He pulled at their cocks greedily. Their kiss intensified. Darryl gripped François' balls, who in turn massaged Michael's cock. First Darryl's thighs tensed and he groaned, never breaking his kiss. He came hard, covering Michael's toned body. Then François threw his head back.

"Oh oui, fais moi venir."

His orgasm exploded over Michael as he cried out, gripping Michael's cock hard. Michael was close and didn't want to wait anymore. Darryl roughly replaced François' hand and kept up the pressure.

Michael tensed his body and let the feeling overwhelm him. Just as François locked lips with him, he came, his body giving itself up to the waves of pleasure.

After they had cleaned themselves, they curled up on the big bed. Darryl lay in the middle with his arms around them.

"That was always going to happen," he murmured.

Michael had lusted after both men since first laying eyes on them, never expecting he'd be with either. Certainly not at the same time. "If that is what guests can expect when they book in here, you'll do a roaring trade."

"Darryl likes to christen every property," François added.

Michael didn't know what that meant. Was that all they saw him as? A local diversion? Suddenly the real world came rushing in. Matthew, Will, everything.

He got off the bed and searched for his clothes.

"Hey, what are you doing?" Darryl asked.

"I'm going to sleep. It's been a mad few days."

"But we've only just started. There's plenty of night left. You can sleep tomorrow."

Darryl looked genuinely concerned, but Michael detected a hint of triumph in François' eyes.

"Thank you for everything, honestly. I'll see you in the morning."

He practically ran out of the room.

Chapter Eight

The next day and François' head was pounding. "I'm sorry, I'm going to have to call you back." He terminated the call and slammed the phone down. The noise of the chainsaw seemed to be making everything jangle, including his nerves.

He walked out through the kitchen onto the terrace, only to be greeted by the sight of Michael crawling around the bloody oak tree he hadn't stopped banging on about. Darryl stood at the bottom holding the ladders, staring up at him like a puppy dog.

Thankfully the noise stopped when they both saw François' face of thunder.

"I've had to cut the call with the bloody architect because of this," François exclaimed.

Darryl frowned at him. "I'm sure they will understand that getting this down is important," he said. "Or do you want the squirrels in your room too?"

The patio flags were covered in sawdust and old bits of branch. François doubted very much Darryl would be picking up a sweeping brush.

"I'm not cleaning this up," François said. "In fact, I'm sticking firmly to my sodding job description from now on. You can change your own bed."

"Don't worry. There won't be a trace when I've finished," Michael said, coming to the bottom of the ladder.

With his hair all over the place and in his worker outfit, he looked so hot. François thought about his naked body and his cock responded. They had slept with some handsome men across the world, but Michael had something different about him. It had puzzled François for quite some time, but this morning he had worked it out. Michael didn't have a clue how attractive he was.

Michael went over to one of the branches to separate it, ready to be chopped into kindling.

"Michael is saying he's going to leave us," Darryl said, wandering over to François. It was almost a whine.

This gardener had the strangest effect on Darryl and François did not approve.

"Maybe it's for the best," he said with the sweetest smile he could muster. "If he's not comfortable here. The last thing you want is someone staying under duress."

"I would rather make him comfortable, so he didn't stay under duress," Darryl returned, irritably.

I bet you would.

He could see he was fighting a losing game. When Darryl fixated on getting something, nothing in the world could stop him. François' job had always been to make sure he got those things in his sights. Any deviation to that could be dangerous.

François sighed and went over to Michael. "Could I have a word?"

He twisted one branch from another. François could imagine his muscles rippling under there and struggled to focus for a second.

"Michael, could I have a word please?"

This time he straightened up. Despite it being a cold day, sweat beaded on his forehead, matting his hair. "What is it?"

François shifted from one foot to the other. "Darryl tells me that you are talking about leaving."

"Not talking. I said I'd do this for you. Then I'll pack my bags."

François fiddled with a twig he'd picked up. "Is it because of what I said last night?"

The other man reddened. "Yes," he said quietly.

The pain on Michael's face sent guilt flooding through François. His viper tongue was legendary in the circles they moved in, but everyone knew it contained no venom. Not really. But he had obviously hurt Michael's feelings.

"Michael. I can be a vicious queen. I say things without a filter. You shouldn't listen to me, honestly."

Michael stared at him. He tried to imagine how he looked through the other man's eyes and didn't like it.

"Half the time I think I'm being funny," François continued. "And the other it's purely thoughtlessness. I'm genuinely sorry. Please won't you stay?"

The other man seemed lost in thought. "You sure you're not just saying it because Darryl put you up to it?"

For someone who seemed to be all about manual labour, Michael was perceptive.

"Of course not," François lied. "I like having you around too. He would have me work from morning to night given half a chance. Consider it an act of humanitarian mercy."

Michael sighed and rubbed his eyes. He looked tired.

"If you're definitely okay with it, then I'd love to stay. The workmen haven't even been out to do a quote for my roof and the last thing Will needs is me pushing him. I'm presuming he's the owner of the cottage now. Who knows? I haven't had chance to ask him."

"Then it's settled," François said, clapping him on the shoulder.

"But perhaps it's best if I stay in my own room," Michael decided. "I think it's dangerous if we get things too mixed up."

"Whatever you need," François said with a warm smile.

* * * *

Michael dragged François' tight boxer shorts off and gripped his hard cock. The rough hands that did outdoor work were surprisingly gentle as they stroked him. François lay on Darryl's bare chest.

Slowly playing with François' cock, Michael bent down and licked the tip. François needed more. He would be begging Michael to put it in his mouth soon.

Darryl tweaked his nipple, sending shockwaves through his body.

"You want it?" Michael asked, feigning innocence.

"*Oui*," François managed.

Michael plunged down, opening wide and taking the whole of François' cock in his mouth. François' body convulsed as the relief took over. Michael wasn't resting on his laurels and sucked the length of François. Reaching up, he took hold of Darryl's hands, who responded by nibbling at his neck.

In no time, François feared he would come and gently stopped Michael. "Not yet," he whispered.

He faced Darryl and kissed him hard. Darryl let his hand drop down to the small of François' back. Michael had moved round to the other side of Darryl and teased his nipple with his teeth.

"You two put on quite a show," Darryl said.

"We're not just here for your amusement," François replied. "I think it's time you played fair."

Darryl shifted on the pillow. "Is that right? And how do you propose I do that?"

François let a wry smile spread across his face. "Turn over, Mr Big Shot."

Darryl obeyed and lay on his front. Michael hesitated for a second. This lack of confidence had been attractive at first but was now irritating François, who had never suffered from such an affliction.

"*Bon appetite*," he said.

Thankfully, Michael didn't need any more urging and buried his face in Darryl's muscular arse. Darryl responded by spreading his legs wide, giving Michael full access. François loved watching Michael enjoying himself.

He lazily massaged his own cock. He liked to be in charge in the bedroom. Sometimes he thought it were the only part of his life that he did have control over.

Eventually, Michael came up for air, wiping his mouth. "That is an amazing arse," he exclaimed.

François got off the bed and retrieved condoms and lube from his wash bag. He came up behind the kneeling Michael, making sure his own erection pushed against him. Reaching around, he slid the condom onto Michael's hard cock.

"Enjoy it then," he whispered in his ear.

Michael let him squeeze lube onto his fingers before probing Darryl's shining hole, Darryl shifting to give him more access. As he did so, François squeezed more lube onto Michael's cock. He slid it over, getting it ready.

Gently pushing him forward, Michael guided his cock into Darryl who raised himself up on his hands and knees. François stood at the end of the bed, watching Michael luxuriating at being inside Darryl. They looked so horny. Michael found a rhythm that, judging by the noises Darryl made into the pillow, was hitting the right spot already.

Michael leaned over, kissing Darryl's neck as he fucked him. Darryl reached behind, gripping him.

Suddenly François didn't like being the outsider and got back onto the bed. Darryl moved and sucked François' cock. Darryl knew exactly how he liked it. Michael fucked Darryl hard now and François matched his momentum as he slid his dick in and out of Darryl's mouth.

"Oh fuck," Michael exclaimed, then let out a cry. François could see him gripping Darryl's waist as his body trembled.

François wasn't far behind him, and he came with a shudder, his cum filling Darryl's mouth and his body wracked with pleasure.

They collapsed onto the bed. Darryl was still hard, and Michael couldn't wait to oblige him. He leant down and sucked greedily. François ran his hands over Darryl's body and kissed him. But he was too late.

Darryl arched his back, running his fingers through Michael's hair.

"Oh yeah, I'm coming."

With a yell, Darryl closed his eyes as Michael swallowed every drop of his cum. For once, François felt uneasy. It was not an emotion that came naturally to him.

"I'm jumping in the shower," he said.

Once in the en suite, he let the hot water cascade over his body. He couldn't understand this. They had done this a hundred times before. He liked Michael as well. Usually, the playthings were after free hotel stays or to be paid, but Michael wasn't like that.

Once he'd finished, he dried his body and resolved that he would make more of an effort. Darryl hated it when he sulked. Returning to the bedroom, he frowned that the bed lay empty. He put on one of Darryl's fluffy bathrobes and went in search of them.

Thorpe Hall might be a big house, but it didn't take long to trace the muffled voices coming from the kitchen. François grinned to himself. It had been years since he'd had a midnight feast. He crept down and was about to make them jump when he overheard the conversation.

"I don't think he likes me," Michael said.

"He practically guided your cock into my arse. What more do you need?" Darryl replied.

François could hear them clattering plates. No doubt they would leave the mess for him to clear up.

"I guess I'm just a bit paranoid. I didn't have many friends growing up."

"Really? That surprises me. I thought your milkshake would have brought all the boys to the yard."

"They didn't really like it when I didn't have any interest in cars or girls. Where did you grow up?"

François wondered how truthful Darryl would be at this point. He usually avoided questions on his past. Only François knew the whole truth. Something he was inordinately proud of.

"I grew up in care," Darryl announced.

François' stomach dropped. Not even some members of the board were privy to this. Now Darryl was giving it up to the gardener. *He must have a magical cock.*

"Really? That must have been hard," Michael soothed.

"I suppose. When you don't know anything else, does it make that much difference?"

"I guess that's where the drive comes from."

Another clatter as they raided the leftovers that were supposed to be for lunch tomorrow. François wanted to go in and join them, but something stopped him.

"Got it in one," Darryl continued. "I vowed I'd never let anything pass me by."

"Well, it worked out for you."

"Did it?"

"What do you mean?"

François frowned.

"What's the point in all this with no one to share it with?" Darryl continued.

"Ah the age-old question, eh? Can you have it all?" Michael replied.

The sound of stools being scraped against the slate floor meant they were on the move. François stole across the landing and into the lounge, leaving the door ajar a little.

"Should we get François something?" Michael said as they came through the door and went into the study where the fire would still be burning.

"Nah, he'll be in the shower for ages yet. Catholic guilt."

Michael let out a guffaw. "Bit late for that."

They shut the door behind them. François walked across the moonlit room and sank down on the sofa. Doubt gnawed at him as he replayed the conversation over in his head.

Something which transcended sex had connected them. He would have to keep a very firm eye on Michael Fleming. Composing himself, he put a smile on and made his way through to the study.

Chapter Nine

A couple of weeks passed, and they had got into quite a nice groove. Michael would spend his days researching plants and making plans while François and Darryl worked in the study.

Michael had been touched when they had both insisted on attending Matthew's funeral. He suspected it was more Darryl's gesture than François'. Michael couldn't work him out. In bed, they were all so compatible, but when Darryl was out of range, Michael detected a cold edge. Nothing major, but it always seemed to be there.

Darryl, on the other hand, Michael found incredibly easy to be around. He seemed to genuinely be interested in Michael and his story. All three of them had shared some wonderful meals and chats by the fire. Michael was probably a little bit in awe of Darryl.

Dragged from his thoughts, he heard Darryl calling his name.

"Michael," he shouted again. "Quick."

Panic setting in, he dashed out of the lounge to the hallway. He found Darryl standing at the front door he'd flung wide open. The cold snap from the air invaded the warm house.

"Look," Darryl said pointing.

Snow fell heavily over Napthwaite. It had already started to settle on the lawn that lined the driveway. He joined Darryl at the door and took in the beauty of it all. The sky was low and grey, which meant it would be snowing for a while yet.

"Where's François?" he asked, putting his hand on Darryl's shoulder.

"Checking we have enough cheese and wine to last the rest of the winter." Darryl placed his own hand on top of Michael's.

Almost mesmerised, they watched the snow cascading over the valley.

"It's beautiful," Darryl said.

Michael wriggled free. "I'm getting François. He can't miss this."

He left Darryl to watch nature's show and made his way through to the kitchen. There he found François breaking pieces of chocolate into a bowl. "What are you doing?" he asked.

François jumped. "I thought we might all like some real hot chocolate. Better than the packet muck that heathen sells in her shop of hideousness."

Michael dashed over to him and took his hand. "Come and watch."

"But..."

Michael planted a kiss on his lips. François took a step back. "You do everything for him. Come and do something for yourself," Michael said.

Before he could reply, he gestured to him to go out of the room. They joined Darryl at the door.

"C'est beau."

All three huddled together for warmth, transfixed on the winter wonderland forming before their very eyes. Once they could take no more and François' teeth were chattering, they reluctantly closed the door.

"It's bloody freezing," François said, rubbing his arms.

"Maybe that's because you insist on wearing a shirt instead of a thick jumper," Darryl teased.

François always had a designer shirt on. Michael couldn't understand it. He lived in his fisherman's sweater and cargo pants. Darryl equally seemed uninterested in fashion. He had some lovely clothes, which Michael suspected François had bought, but he always opted for the same sweater and jeans.

His thoughts were interrupted by a notification on his phone that he'd received a message. He glanced down at it.

Snow's settling. Come up to the farm. Sledges for all. Ed x

Michael looked at the other two eagerly.

"What's with you?" Darryl asked.

"Oh, nothing you'd be interested in, I shouldn't think. I'm heading out. Ed's invited me over for a sledge."

Darryl glanced at a horrified François. "Just you?" he asked.

Michael glanced down at the message again.

"He says 'sledges for all'."

"How about we gate-crash?" Darryl said. "I haven't been sledging in years."

"I have never been sledging." François sniffed. "I went skiing as a child. I suppose it's the same thing."

"Oh, come on, grumpy," Darryl said, flinging an arm around him. "You might have fun."

They got decked out in their warmest clothes, even managing to persuade François to put on one of Michael's jumpers.

"Very rugged," Darryl announced when they regrouped at the door.

François returned his jolly observation with a scowl. "I feel like I should be singing Christmas carols by a fireside."

"Come on," Michael said.

He loved snow. Growing up on the south coast, it had been a stranger to him as a child. They hurried down the road towards the village. Michael cringed when he saw his poor cottage.

"Any idea when it will be safe for you?" François asked.

"The workmen managed to get all the tree stuff out and secure the roof last week."

"That sounds positive," Darryl said.

"Yeah. It's slow going though. They'll need to replace most of the tiles now. This weather won't help."

They turned onto Queen Street. It seemed like all the villagers were out and heading in the same direction.

"Michael."

He looked up to see Mrs Turnbull in a window above the newsagents. She'd been staying with Kathleen Brockbank since the night of the storm.

"Hello, Mrs T. How are you?"

"Not coming out in that," she announced. "The doctor who did my hip last year would have my guts for garters."

"Can I get you anything from the shop?" he asked.

"You're so kind. I miss you being next door. No, nothing for me, I just saw you passing and wanted to say hello."

"I miss you too, Mrs T. Especially your coffee cake."

She winked at him. "Kathleen's kitchen isn't very well stocked. I'll see what I can do, though."

"Bessie Turnbull," Kathleen shouted from inside the room. "Shut that window. I'm not paying to heat the bloody street."

Mrs Turnbull rolled her eyes and shut the window. She gave them a wave before they carried on walking up Queen Street, out of the village.

"You know everyone in this village?" François asked.

"Pretty much," Michael replied. "I've been here about a year now. It's hard not to."

"We've been here a month and only know you," Darryl added.

François skidded on a bit of ice. Michael steadied him.

"They know you though," Michael continued. "You're that kind man who put everyone up in the storms and who is going to breathe new life into the Hall."

Whoops and cries could be heard over the still winter air.

"Come on," Michael said, breaking into a trot.

They dashed through the woods and past Christine Carrington's cottage.

"Look," Darryl exclaimed.

The field above Ed's farm was full of people. Nearly every villager had come out to play. With joy like children on Christmas morning, Darryl and Michael dashed up the farm track. François followed at a brisk walk.

Once they reached the field, Michael couldn't believe the scene. It could have been a Christmas card come to life. Villagers were racing one another down the field. So many tracks had been carved out already that it looked like a lattice-topped pie. Parents with smaller children were building snowmen and snowball fights were breaking out all over the field. It was perfect.

Ed came over, beaming, when he saw them standing at the gate. "Isn't it brilliant? We used to do this when we were kids."

"Who organised it?" Darryl asked.

"No one," Ed laughed. "It just happened. This is the best field for sledging in the whole of Yorkshire. Come on."

They followed Ed to the top of the hill. Ed's beautiful border collie, Madge, came for a fuss. The field was full of dogs. Madge gave the impression she knew this was her realm and she must act accordingly.

"We haven't got a sledge," Michael said.

"No bother. There's a ton of them. If people are having a rest, they just chuck them down there."

"How very communal," François muttered.

Michael stared at him. He had disdain written all over his face. "We have a virgin here, Ed."

François jolted as all eyes fell on him. "I've been skiing," he said.

"Not the same," Ed answered. "Maybe you should go over there. There's a smaller hill. Arthur is in there with his class."

Michael tried his best to hide his face as outrage crept over François' face.

"Are you suggesting I ride with infants?"

"I just thought…"

"Come on," Michael said, taking François' arm. "I'll take you for your first ride."

"It's been a while since anyone said that," Darryl said with a smirk. "You kids have fun. I'll be watching."

Michael and François walked over to the sledges. A huge snowball fight had distracted a lot of people, so they had quite the choice. Michael selected a long red one. "This okay?"

François nodded.

"You're not nervous, are you?" Michael asked.

"Pah," he retorted. "Of course I'm not. There is nothing you can ride that I can't."

Michael laughed. "Time to put that theory to the test, big boy."

They walked to the top of the hill. A couple of young lads with alarmingly ruddy cheeks nearly knocked them over.

"It seems like a good run," Michael said as he watched them scoot down the hillside.

"I'm only doing this because Darryl would tease me otherwise." François sniffed. "If my mother could see me now, she would be horrified."

François had never spoken about his family before, and Michael was intrigued. But it wasn't time for a chat. Standing at the top of the hill, it was a lot steeper than it had seemed from below.

"Do you want to go in front or behind?" he asked, painfully aware of the double entendre in his words.

"So far, I've only seen you behind, so let's stick with that. For now," François replied.

His words were equally laden with meaning. Michael had topped both Darryl and François, but he hadn't bottomed for either. In his mind all he could see François' huge cock. It would be a challenge.

"Are we doing this or what?" François had got onto the front of the sledge and was staring up at him expectantly. Michael slid in behind him and wrapped his arms around his waist. François leant against him.

"Ready?" Michael said into his ear.

François gripped onto his arms. "I was born ready, Michael Fleming," he replied.

With a kick, Michael launched the sledge off the ridge, and they hit the steep decline with force. He realised he'd probably given it a bit too much strength as their weight gave the little craft speed.

François let out a whoop of exhilaration as they sped past other villagers. Michael held on to him tightly as they reached the bottom of the hill.

But they didn't stop and were headed straight for the boggy pond in the corner of the field.

"Bail!" Michael shouted.

He and François rolled off the sledge, into the snow, ending up in a tangle of limbs. The next thing, François' lips were on him, kissing him furiously. When they broke and got up, François' face was flushed. "That was bloody brilliant. Can we go again?"

"Too bloody right we can." Michael giggled.

The sledge had carried itself over to the pond.

"I'll get it," François announced, happily scampering off.

Darryl came over. "Everyone has a child locked inside. Even the Ice Queen herself."

Michael hadn't seen such unbridled joy on François' face before. It suited him. "What about you? You up for a ride?"

"I'm always up for a ride," Darryl replied. "Do you think all three of us would fit on?"

Michael stared at him. "We fit quite well in other places. I don't see why not."

They wandered over to the foot of the hill. James and Ed were at the top in sledges. Arthur counted them down before they set off, racing to the finish line.

"They seem very happy, don't they?" Darryl said.

"Yes. I guess finding a love that works means everything."

Ed beat James to the finish line and rewarded him with a big handful of snow down the back of his jacket. James in turn, rugby tackled Ed, so they were rolling in the snow.

"You can see who the adult in that relationship is," Michael said, pointing to the top of the hill.

Arthur stood shaking his head with a look of love in his eyes. The younger of the three by a long chalk, but today he could only spectate.

"Who is the adult in our relationship?" Darryl asked.

Michael snapped to attention. "Our...?"

"Sorry, ignore me. I didn't mean—"

"Come on, you two. Let's go again," François shouted from the bottom of the hill.

Darryl dashed off to join him.

Michael watched him go. What on earth did he mean?

Chapter Ten

"Will you stop bloody fussing? I'm fine."

"My eyes must be deceiving me then, because you look as rough as a cow's arse."

"Thank you very much."

Darryl let out a loud sneeze. François pulled another tissue from the box and handed it to him. With a face like thunder, Darryl took it and blew his nose.

"I'll cancel your meetings today. You're going nowhere."

"Ugh. I never get ill."

"You are now. I bloody said going out in the snow was a bad idea. My poor delicate little flower."

Darryl smiled up at him. "We had fun though, didn't we?"

François had to admit that it had been fun. They had gone down that hill ten times or more and each time had been as much fun as the first one.

"What's Michael doing?" Darryl asked.

Can he not let his new plaything out of his sight? "He's in the small library-study, staring at those gardening books, again. I don't know what he finds so fascinating in them. Once you've seen a flower, it's pretty much the same as the next."

"It's his passion. Like I'm yours."

"Dream on. Now I'd best go and cancel my passion's commitments today. I'll tell them you're at death's door and the strain could very well tip you into oblivion."

"Wait a second. Do you think Michael is still working on plans for this place?"

He nodded. He'd peeped over his shoulder the day before and seen sketches of the grounds. He had been meaning to mention it. "I do. You're going to have to speak to him."

Darryl groaned. "I will, just not today. I think maybe I should have a sleep."

François pulled the duvet over him. "You could put some pyjamas on too."

Darryl beamed up at him. "If I'm feeling better later, you two could show me your bedside manner."

"Bed is for rest today, Mr Burlington. Sorry to disappoint you, but I wouldn't go near your body fluids for a million pounds."

Darryl winked. "You would."

François left him to it and went downstairs to the study. On the way, he glanced in at Michael in the smaller study-reading room. He was totally engrossed in a load of books. They were being unfair, letting him create wonderful plans when they knew it would be a car park in a year's time.

He also knew that Darryl would be expecting him to do the dirty work. As usual.

François shut himself in the study they were using as an office and got on with cancelling Darryl's appointments and dealing with emails from Kefalonia as well as more local suppliers. Work would begin on Thorpe Hall soon. The cat would be out of the bag then.

Bloody Kefalonia. Darryl still wanted him to go and supervise the opening. He wondered what would happen if Michael and Darryl were left to their own devices. Maybe he should think of an excuse not to go.

The afternoon passed, and he made a thick broth for them all in the evening. His grandmother had sworn by it when any of her grandchildren had caught a cold. He gave Darryl a double portion. He was feverish and had regressed to being a small boy. At times like this, François loved him the most. Darryl had told him terrible stories about his childhood. François always wanted to fill the hole that had been left with care, when given the chance.

The clock on the stairs struck nine as François collected the dishes from Darryl's room. He was fast asleep, and François stood watching him for a second. He had never met a more remarkable man.

But what is it I want? Why can I never get it?

As usual he shut those thoughts out and went down to the kitchen to load the dishwasher.

"You never stop," Michael said as he came into the room.

"I like to be busy."

On his own with Michael made him uncomfortable. He felt assured with the role Darryl expected him to play when they were all together, but without the key player, he floundered.

"How about we load it up tomorrow? Come and have a brandy."

Never one to refuse a brandy, François followed Michael through to the lounge. He ignored the books still out on the table and sank in a wingback chair by the fire.

Michael prepared the drinks and sat in the other chair across from him, handing him the glass.

"To happy times," Michael said, raising his glass.

"*Salut*," François replied, taking a sip. The liquid stung his lips, but the warmth that travelled down his throat made it worthwhile.

"How is he?" Michael asked.

"Oh, he's fine. It's just a cold. Of course, he's playing to the gallery. He's very good at a dying scene when he's ill."

"I'll stick my head around tomorrow."

"He's also very touchy. You have been warned," François added. "Darryl Burlington gives the original bear with a sore head a run for its money when he's incapacitated."

François studied Michael. He'd seen him in all sorts of positions now, but every time Michael entered a room, his beauty still took François by surprise. Tonight, illuminated by the dancing orange flames of the fire, he looked perfect. François closed his eyes and let out a sigh.

"Tired?"

He opened his eyes to see Michael studying him. "No, I don't do tired. Didn't you know?"

"He's lucky to have you. You're a husband in nearly every sense of the word."

"Some would probably say wife, but I get your meaning," François said, taking another sip.

The fire crackled and Michael leant forward, throwing a log on. The sparks flew up the chimney before settling down into a steady burn.

"How did you meet?" Michael asked, settling into his chair.

"Ah the big question, eh? I'm surprised Darryl hasn't told you."

Michael said nothing. All that could be heard was the clock's dull tick as François worked out where to begin.

"I came to the UK nine years ago with no concrete plan but dreams of being an English teacher. I had read too many novels, I think. Let's face it, the British comprehensive system is not full of little darlings eager to absorb the learning we give them."

Michael snorted. "Quite the culture shock if you were expecting that."

François nodded. His first day in a classroom had resulted in his lunch being stolen, his jacket decorated with obscene messages on Post-its and a mass walk-out when the ice-cream van had driven past.

"I gave it a good go, but it wasn't for me. I wanted more than doing lesson plans while everyone else had fun. I wanted to be where the fun was and took a job in a bar in Compton Street in London."

"I bet you had fun down there," Michael said.

François nodded. In his early twenties, he'd thought he ruled the world. As a Frenchman, he had attracted a lot of interest. "You could say a little too much. Let's say I allowed it to consume me."

"Drugs?"

"Drugs, sex, booze. The lot." He couldn't meet Michael's stare. Strangely he found himself fearing being judged.

"I met Darryl in a sauna in Shoreditch. He recognised me from a film I'd made."

Michael sat up. "You've been in movies?"

François shifted uncomfortably. "Not quite movies but I was in a couple of DVDs. I'm sure I don't need to spell it out to you."

Realisation spread across Michael's face. "Oh, that sort."

"Yes, well I might have a copy upstairs. I'll sign it for you. Anyway, one thing led to another, and we had quite the weekend at his. He mentioned that he needed an assistant and so I went for it."

Michael frowned. "Didn't you want more?"

Annoyance flashed in him. This entitled man had no idea what François wanted.

"Michael, it's all very easy for a man who's won prizes at the Chelsea bloody Flower show. People pay through the nose for your services. I don't have that luxury. Sometimes it isn't about what you want, but about what you need. And what you can give."

His words hung in the air. Darryl always said he needed to soften his edges. Once again, François had proven him right. "I'm sorry if that sounded harsh," he added. "Darryl and I are complicated."

Michael leant forward and put a hand on François' knee. "It's me who should apologise. I had no idea."

To his horror, tears pricked the backs of his eyes.

"Why should you?" He sniffed. "It's not something I make it a habit of advertising."

Michael launched forward and pressed his lips to his. Feeling the muscular bulk of Michael as he crouched between François' legs, his heavy body leaning on him, wad wonderful. So much so that François returned the kiss with a hunger that surprised even him.

He grabbed hold of Michael's corded shoulders and ran his hands through his hair. Michael pulled away, panting.

"Take me to bed," he whispered.

"But…"

"Just take me to bed," he repeated, more insistently.

They practically ran up the stairs, and François' heart hammered wildly by the time they got inside his room. He had almost suggested checking in on Darryl. Then he'd realised that Michael wanted him. Tonight, he wouldn't be Darryl's add-on to make things more spicy.

Once the door was safely shut, he pulled at Michael's clothes. He knew what lay under Michael's thick jumper and jeans, but unwrapping him still gave François chills. Once they were both naked, they fell onto the bed, kissing feverishly, Michael's cock grinding against his.

François ran his hands over Michael's taut biceps then wrapped his legs over his firm butt. They writhed and explored each other as if for the first time.

Michael leant on his haunches and massaged François' cock. He licked the end, letting his saliva coat the head. François relaxed into it. To connect with just one person was wonderful and something he hadn't done for a while.

He gasped as Michael sucked at his balls, taking one, then the other, in his mouth. He gently played with them. The sensation made François cry out for more.

With a grin, Michael traced the bulging vein on the side of François' cock with his tongue then, when he reached the top, he looked up. François locked eyes with him and nodded. The warmth as Michael swallowed his hard dick sent a rush through his whole body. He gripped the sheets and thrust his head into the pillow.

He opened his eyes to see Michael's head bobbing up and down. God he was good at this. To avoid the very real possibility of coming in seconds, François shifted his position, so he pulled Michael's face up to meet his own. Their mouths collided again. He could taste his cock on Michael's tongue.

Reaching under where Michael squatted, François found his hole and ran his finger along it. Michael moaned and shifted to give him better access. François brought his finger up so they both licked at it. Then he returned it to between Michael's legs, slowly rubbing his puckered hole and gently forcing his way inside.

Breaking the kiss, Michael rocked up and down, each movement allowing François farther inside.

"Oh God, yeah," he murmured. In the weeks they'd all been sleeping together, they had never done this. François wanted it all. He wriggled out from under Michael and moved behind him. Pre-empting his thoughts, Michael leant forward onto his hands and knees. His solid arse lay before François, and it was perfect. Wetting his lips, he dove his face in between Michael's cheeks. The yelp that Michael gave as François licked hard made François' cock twitch even more.

He lapped at him hungrily, pulling his cheeks apart to get better access. Michael cried out. "Oh God, give me more."

"I want to fuck you," François panted.

Michael moved onto his back and stared at François' huge cock with a little trepidation. "It's been a while and—"

"Relax," François murmured. "I'll be gentle."

"Safe words are 'get the fuck off me', okay?"

François laughed. "Okay." He reached into his washbag and rolled a condom on before liberally applying lube. "You have me so turned on, I'll probably only last a few seconds," he said.

Michael raised his legs onto François' shoulders. "Once you're in, you'd better fuck me good," he dared him.

François had never shied away from a challenge and tonight would be no exception. He positioned himself and slowly pushed his way inside. The look on Michael's face made him even more turned on, if that were possible. At first, Michael cried out. Then as François slid inside, he relaxed, and his eyes became heavy.

"Oh God, that's good," he sighed.

"Permission to fuck you good?" François said, licking the inside of Michael's calf.

"Permission granted," Michael said.

François began to fuck him. He let him get used to the motion first before building up. He grabbed Michael's ankles and spread his legs wide apart, giving him as much access as he could get. "Jesus, you are so hot," he said.

Michael pulled at his own cock as François dived in and out of him. He let Michael's legs go and fell onto his face, still bucking his hips as their tongues met. Michael wrapped his legs around François' waist, and they melded together as two halves of one coin.

Using his body weight, Michael rolled them over in the bed and straddled François. He rode him so hard the bed banged against the wall. But at that point neither of them cared. They were on a mission with only one resolution.

"Oh fuck, ride me. Make me come," François grunted.

This made Michael pick up the pace. Despite the cold night outside, sweat coursed down his chest. François leaned up and ran his finger through it, licking and tasting his salt.

"Don't stop. I'm coming," Michael cried out. He bent over almost double and moaned. Just as his cum hit François' chest, his arse contracted around François' cock. Seconds later, François came with force. He dug his nails into Michael's thigh as they both let the waves wash over them.

Once they had recovered, Michael gingerly rolled off him. François threw the condom into the bin and went through to the bathroom. Letting the shower burst into life, he stepped under its jets.

"Is it really Catholic guilt?"

He opened his eyes to find Michael watching him.

"Don't listen to everything Darryl tells you," François said dismissively. "There's nothing wrong in being clean."

Michael stepped in and lathered his body up. "Fair point."

Suddenly François felt claustrophobic. What did this man want from him? "There's nothing wrong with privacy either," he muttered.

Michael reached down and squeezed his cock. "I think it's a bit late for that."

Squirming out of his reach, François stepped out of the shower. "Do me a favour?"

Michael turned the shower off and leaned against the wall, his arms folded and an infuriating amused look on his face. "Don't tell me. What just happened stays between us? No blabbing to Darryl."

François threw a towel at him. "Precisely that. I told you, it's complicated."

He left him to dry off and walked into his bedroom. Did he expect them to spend the whole night together? Throwing the towel onto the chair in the corner, he got under the covers. Now all the activity had finished, the cold couldn't be ignored.

Michael came in. "Don't worry, I'll go to my room," he said, gathering his clothes.

François found himself saying, "You don't have to."

Michael got into the bed next to him, wrapping his arm around his waist. François reached up and switched the lamp off, plunging the room into darkness.

"I won't say anything," Michael said, his breath tickling François' ear.

"*Merci.*"

"Not that it's any of his business."

François shifted. He didn't want to psychoanalyse his relationship with Darryl in their sex sheets. "I like to stay one step ahead of him, all right? Otherwise, I'll be gone. Darryl might come across as the kind host, but he can be ruthless. He didn't get to where he is by taking on dead weight."

In the silence that followed, an owl hooted in the woods.

"I think you underestimate how he feels about you," Michael said eventually. "And I know you play down how you feel about him."

François was about to announce that maybe Michael would be better sleeping in his own room when a tear escaped his eye.

"You're in love with him," Michael continued. "Aren't you?"

Whether it was the moonlight dappling the bed, or the aftereffects of great sex, but François couldn't muster the energy to construct his usual shield. "Maybe I am," he said. "Fat lot of good it will do me."

Chapter Eleven

Relentless rain pelted against the windowpanes. Darryl hadn't surfaced for a couple of days, but François and Michael had made their own entertainment.

Michael had quite enjoyed having this time with François. Without Darryl in the room, he revealed a softer side to his nature. He still insisted on being at Darryl's beck and call, though.

As a gardener, Michael hated winter. He loved to be outside, digging and making things better. He had spent quite a bit of time researching books and the internet for plants. Now all he had to do was create the plan for the new garden. It would be sad to lose the beds he had created for Matthew, but it had to be done. They were personal to him and wouldn't be appropriate for a hotel.

He wandered into the lounge to find François lying on the sofa, reading. "Darryl still asleep then?"

François peered over the book. "I think he's getting better. He'll probably be up later and then the fun will start. What are you doing today?"

For what felt like the hundredth time, Michael looked out of the window. "Not sure. I thought about going to visit Will, but it's vile out there. Maybe I'll go anyway. I can't bear being stuck in."

Michael moved François' legs and sat on the couch. "I suppose you're on call all day."

"Sure am. Gives me time to catch up on some reading. I never get chance when his lordship needs a hundred things doing."

"What are you so engrossed in?"

François held up the book, *The Collected Poems of Sylvia Plath*. Michael frowned.

"I didn't have you down as a poetry buff."

Letting the book fall onto his chest, François smiled. "There's a lot you don't know about me. My capacity to shock knows no bounds."

He had a point. Even though he and François had found a more physical connection since Darryl had fallen ill, François resisted most of Michael's attempts at getting to know him better.

"She's buried not far from here. I could take you."

"That would be wonderful," François said, his face lighting up. "When I was younger, I loved her words. I even had my own collection of poems published."

He really was a dark horse. Michael had devoured books ever since he had learnt to read, but poetry had eluded him. Maybe he should give it another go. "Really? That's amazing. I'd love to read them. Were they translated?"

But as soon as the gates had opened, they slammed shut again. François' expression changed to the haughty queen he like to hide behind. He sat up, pulling his feet away from Michael. "No, nothing like that. It was years ago."

Michael reached out and rested his hand on François' knee. "I think that's so impressive. No need to be embarrassed. I bet Darryl has read them."

"Pah," François exclaimed. "He's not interested in poems, and I've never told him. I don't want you opening your big mouth either, thank you very much."

Michael held his hands up in surrender. "Don't worry, your secret is safe with me. But I don't understand. If I'd had a book published, I'd shout it from the rooftops."

"Well, you're not me. People don't want some whimsical Frenchman with a notebook of poems. I reinvented myself."

"People? Or Darryl?"

François shifted again, clearly uneasy at where this conversation had headed.

Michael didn't like to make him uncomfortable. "I'm sorry, that's none of my business."

François got up from the sofa and threw the book in the bin. "You're right. It is none of your business. You've spent a few weeks with us, and you think you have it all worked out. News for you is, you don't."

He made his way towards the door. Michael hated confrontation and he didn't want François thinking he were ungrateful for all they had done for him.

"Please wait. I'm clumsy with my words, I know that."

François stopped at the door and turned, looking past Michael to the window behind him. "It's brightening up out there. I'm sure your friend would enjoy a visit. Don't let us keep you."

Before Michael could reply, François slipped out of the room. Punching the sofa cushion, Michael cursed at his big mouth. His mother had told him many times that his grasp of the English language, or lack of, would get him into trouble. That was why he preferred to say nothing, most of the time.

François was right though. The rain had stopped, and the threat of sunlight seemed to be coming over the fells surrounding the valley. He would go and see Will. Despite its size, Thorpe Hall could be claustrophobic. It had been the same in Matthew's time. Maybe the Hall did something to people. That didn't bode well for a hotel.

On his way out of the room, he leant down and retrieved the book out of the waste bin. Carefully, he laid it on the side table.

* * * *

Will was still staying with Andrew in his cottage on the outskirts of the village. Michael enjoyed the feeling of the icy Yorkshire wind on his face as he walked past the green and up the lane.

He kept thinking about François and his relationship with Darryl. He'd admitted he was probably in love with him. It confused Michael why François had never shown Darryl his true self. Michael wasn't naïve to the ways of the world, but he couldn't understand how people hid themselves. He had always been an open book.

He flinched when he thought about a book. Why had he been so vocal about something that François obviously didn't want to talk about?

As he reached the squeaky gate, Sally, Andrew's black Labrador, barked madly. He made his way up the path.

Hardeep opened the door before Michael even had the chance to knock.

"Hello, Michael."

"Oh hi, Hardeep. I'm not disturbing anything, am I?"

Hardeep laughed. "Of course not. Come in."

Will sat at the dining table. He looked drawn and thinner than usual, which was saying something. Michael wished he'd given him more attention instead of sleeping with the two newcomers.

"I'll be off then," Hardeep said.

"Not on my account, I hope," Michael replied, sitting at the table next to Will.

Hardeep shook his head. "I promised Satinder I'd take her clothes shopping to Leeds. Now her mother has buggered off to Spain again, it's down to me." He kissed Will and ran his hands through his hair. "Sure, you don't want to come? Satinder would love to see you."

Will took hold of Hardeep's hand and kissed the back of it. "No thanks, babe. But tell her to spend every penny of those vouchers we got her."

Hardeep put his coat on.

"Try to get him out," he said to Michael. "It's stuffy in here. He needs some fresh air."

"He's also not deaf," Will muttered.

Hardeep kissed him again. "But he never listens to me so maybe you'll have better luck. I'll see you later." Patting Michael on the shoulder as he walked by, Hardeep let himself out. They heard the familiar gate-squeak that meant he'd gone.

Will exhaled loudly.

"Before you say anything, if it's an attempt to force me to feel better, don't."

Michael swallowed his words immediately.

Will's face softened. "I'm sorry. I love Hardeep and Andrew. Honestly, I do. I feel like the luckiest man in the world sometimes. But I don't want to feel better. I want to wallow. Am I not allowed that?"

"You're allowed whatever you need," Michael replied. "We all think we know what's best for people but how can we? Not really."

Will narrowed his eyes. "Now that sounds intriguing. I get the impression you're not talking about my love life. What's going on in my childhood home?"

Michael had never had a filter and he'd never been able to lie. Even though he had come to visit Will, the uncertainty of his feelings for Darryl and François bubbled so furiously inside him that he couldn't keep a lid on it. "I slept with Darryl and François, then I slept with François and now I'm all sorts of confused."

The surprise on Will's face almost made Michael laugh out loud.

"This calls for a bottle of wine." Will got up to get one from the kitchen, but Michael caught his arm.

"I'm sorry. I came here to talk about you. Forget I said anything."

"Oh, Michael. I've spoken about nothing but me since the night of the storm. This sounds juicy and the distraction is like a gift from God." He bustled into the kitchen and the pop of a cork could be heard. Will returned with two glasses of prosecco and the bottle that he plonked firmly down on the table. Sitting, he clinked his glass with Michael's and took a long sip. "Now tell Uncle Will all about it. Leave nothing out."

They made light work of the bottle of wine as Michael recounted the events of the last couple of weeks. Will seemed to be hanging on his words and responding perfectly well to a conversation that didn't feature his father or his lovers. He drained the bottle into their glasses and scurried into the kitchen for another.

"I can't be drunk when I get to the Hall," Michael shouted after him.

"Nonsense. You can do what you like. You're a big boy and sounds like they know that now."

Michael blushed as Will returned to his seat with a fresh bottle that he opened with gusto. "So, what's the problem with it all then?" he asked.

Michael stretched. "Oh, I don't know. Their relationship is a mess. François is in love with Darryl, and I reckon Darryl feels the same way. At least a little bit. But then I get these vibes from both of them towards me."

Will took a swig from his glass. "Have them both then. Look at Andrew, Hardeep and me. I might be going through hell at the moment, but in a weird way, I've also never been happier. Does that make me a terrible person?"

Michael shook his head. "Not at all. Things aren't always good or bad. Life is more complicated than that."

"Then...?"

"Then what? Declare my undying love for them and watch as they throw all my stuff out onto the drive?"

Will shook his head. "That might be a bit extreme. See how things play out. Get to know them more. If you still feel it's a danger zone, you've lost nothing."

Michael thought about living and working with people he was sleeping with. It had all the hallmarks of disaster.

"There's still something wrong? What is it?"

He hated talking to Will about this as Matthew had taken responsibility for his predicament, but he didn't have anyone else. "It's the work side," he said. "I've asked them a few times about the future. It will be spring soon and I'll need to start work when the weather fairs up. I've done a shitload of research, but they aren't giving me anything solid." He hoped he hadn't upset Will by making him think of Matthew. "I'm sorry, it's not your—"

"Michael, you're my friend. Let's give all that apologising shit up. I think you should force their hand on that one."

"How?"

"Draw up the plans and make a proper appointment to present them. Make it clear that work and bed are two completely separate lives. They need to understand that you aren't some bloody plaything."

Instantly Michael thought about François' catty comments the first night they had slept together. "Maybe that is what I am to them. They'll be gone in the spring, and I'm left with nothing."

"Then all the more reason to find out now."

Chapter Twelve

For the first day in ages, Darryl resembled something vaguely human again. After standing in the shower for what seemed like an hour, he threw on some jeans and a sweater. His reflection in the mirror told him he still looked rough, but he'd grown sick of the room François had practically locked him in.

Hearing voices downstairs, he made his way to the kitchen. François and Michael were just finishing up breakfast. They were mid-conversation about something which stopped when they saw him enter the room.

"Look who it is," Michael exclaimed.

He was just as handsome as ever. Darryl's cock tingled at his presence. He was most certainly on the road to recovery.

François leapt off his stool and ushered Darryl over as if he'd just woken from a decade-long coma. "Can I get you anything?" he asked, worry etched across his face.

Darryl appreciated all the care he'd given him, but it had begun to feel suffocating. "Just some coffee."

François bustled off to make him a drink. Darryl pulled a face at Michael.

"Good to see you're feeling better," Michael said, eating the last piece of his toast.

Darryl stretched. "Fighting fit and raring to go. What have I missed?"

"Not much. Except Mrs Turnbull is in this month's *Playboy*, the Poole woman has won an award for her endless charity work and Harvey Nichols are considering buying the village hall to open a flagship store," François said. He put a steaming mug of coffee down in front of Darryl, which he fell on. He needed this. "Are you working today?"

Darryl considered this as he blew on the hot drink. "Maybe later. Did the swatches for the curtains in the bungalows come?"

"Yesterday. Plus, we have samples of cutlery to go through. Six boxes."

"Have mercy on me. What are you doing today?" he asked Michael.

A look of evasiveness came over him. "Oh, just some bits and bobs. In fact, I'd better get cracking. Am I all right having the lounge again?"

"Sure. Don't forget coffee and pastries at ten," François said breezily.

Michael mock saluted and left the room. François hopped up onto his now vacant stool.

"You two are getting on well," Darryl commented.

"Not jealous, are you?" François asked.

"Of whom?" Darryl retorted.

François hummed to himself and thumbed through a gardening magazine that Michael had left behind. "Your new plaything, of course."

Darryl sipped his coffee. The rocket fuel that François made was just what he needed today. He might be feeling better but wasn't one hundred percent. A couple of these would fire him up nicely. "I've no doubt you've been keeping him entertained."

The smug grin on François' face told him they had most certainly been getting to know each other in every way. But jealousy did wash over him and for some strange reason, he wasn't sure of whom. Darryl Burlington did not give in to insecurities, but the idea of these two having sex all night while he lay fast asleep made him feel surplus to requirements. That was a feeling he didn't like.

"Can you get us a list of things to go through in order of priority?" he snapped.

François raised an eyebrow. "Sure thing, boss. What time do you want to go through it?"

"Give me an hour."

Picking up his coffee, Darryl left the room. Standing out in the hall, he tried to understand why he'd reacted like that. He wasn't a spare part—he owned the fucking place. Not ready for another knowing look from François, he crossed the hall and made his way into the lounge. There he found Michael, surrounded by books spread out on the table that sat in the window. It gave a beautiful view of the garden.

Michael was so engrossed that he didn't hear Darryl come in, so Darryl walked carefully over to him. Peering over his shoulder, Darryl could see that Michael was sketching a plan on a huge piece of white paper. To his horror, the plan was for Thorpe Hall.

What shit has François been filling his head with?

"Very impressive," he said.

Michael jumped and spun around. "Darryl. I didn't hear you come in."

Perching down on the chair next to Michael, he studied the plans. "I creep like a stealthy cat." He smiled. "Talk me through these."

Michael spent the next half an hour telling Darryl what they could do with the gardens at Thorpe Hall. He had come up with ingenious ways to grow produce for the kitchen. Darryl had no idea they could create so much in a small space.

Then he'd designed little walks for guests with almost-hidden bistro tables that would give the impression of a secret garden. Once they'd cleared the buildings, the main grounds were still mainly lawns, but Michael had brought in shrubs and identified some wonderful sculptures that would give the view texture.

Darryl had that familiar tingle in his body that he got when he loved an idea. "What's this down here?" he asked, pointing to some sketches right at the boundary fence where the beck ran along from the village.

"Ah, that is a barbeque and performance area. I thought it would be nice to have lectures or small theatre presentations down there. If guests weren't interested, I'm sure villagers would be. If the budget would stretch, we could even get an awning."

"I love it."

Michael reddened around the neck as Darryl went over every inch of the plan again, to check he hadn't missed anything. The extent of Michael's talent bowled him over. He'd done good work on the gardens of Thorpe Hall, but Darryl had assumed Matthew had been the creative brains behind the project. Now he doubted this.

"I'd ideally like to get the go-ahead soon, Darryl," Michael said, not looking up from the plan. "I need to make a start ordering stock, and we might need landscapers to do some bits. It would make sense to get them in at the same time as the builders. Save on the mess."

Darryl drained his cup. "Leave it with me. You are so talented, Michael. Why are you hiding your light up here?"

Michael threw a pencil down on the desk. "I did the Chelsea thing and creating little urban paradises for the rich folk of London. Not my style. I want to create things that will be here long after I'm gone. That people will instantly say 'That's a Michael Fleming'."

Darryl glanced at the plans. He certainly had a signature style. It had been unfair of them to let Michael pursue this. Picking up his mug, Darryl headed over to the door. "I'll get you an answer this week. I promise."

As he walked into the hall, François was barking instructions at someone over the phone. Darryl followed the harsh tones to find François in the study, sitting by the fire with a laptop on his knee.

"We need non-branded napkin rings. I told you that. Burlington Hotels will not be advertising your business every time they lay a table. What kind of place do you think we're running? Get them changed." He slammed the lid down. "These people are imbeciles," he announced.

Darryl loved it when François took the world on. "They won't be when you've finished with them." He commandeered the other leather wingback chair that sat across from the one François occupied. They looked like two very different gargoyles, guarding a fire that was still to be lit.

"You feeling okay?" François asked. "I don't have a window in the diary for you to keel over."

"I'm fine, honestly. Whatever I had is long gone."

Seemingly satisfied, François flipped open the laptop. "The list is big. You might want another caffeine hit."

"I thought we had coffee and pastries at ten?"

François reddened. "Ignoring that. Where do you want to start? Bedrooms or public areas?"

"Gardens."

François frowned up at him. "What are you talking about?"

"Michael has done some impressive work. Have you seen it?"

"Of course not. What is the point?"

"So, you just let him spend God knows how long in there on a wild-goose chase?"

François huffed and put the laptop screen down with a bang. Darryl made a note to take it out of his wages if he broke it. "I don't know about any bloody wild geese. What I do know is, while you were at death's door, your new pet needed occupying, your business had to carry on and you seemed to require soup and sympathy on an hourly basis. As flattering as your assumption that I am a superhero is, I'm not."

He had a point. "Fine. I apologise for taking you for granted. Anyway, I've had a look at some of his plans, and they are amazing."

"I'm sure they are. He's a very creative and accomplished man."

Darryl felt decidedly ill when a misty look swept over François' face as he said this. "So why don't we go for it?"

"Because our plans say that has to be a car park, remember?"

Darryl sighed. As he'd lain in bed, coughing and spluttering, he'd realised how beautiful the room was with its oak panels and coving. Their new plans would have it as storerooms. Most of the accommodation would be in the new builds.

"When we've finished, there will be no bedrooms in the Hall," he said, mostly to himself. "Not one person will sleep in this Hall again after us. It's a strange feeling, isn't it?"

François sighed. "These were the plans you approved in London. What are you saying?"

"I'm thinking aloud. Can I afford this place if I buy it off Burlington?"

"No," François replied sharply.

"I bet I can. I could sell the London house easily."

François shifted in his seat. "You must still be ill. Are you seriously talking about living here?" He looked around as if they were in a slum instead of a beautiful old Hall.

"Why not? Imagine this as a statement of my success."

"And you could keep a handsome gardener at your disposal?"

François could see right through him as usual.

The clock struck ten.

"Ah, it must be coffee and pastries time," Darryl said, leaping up.

A sulky François followed him through into the kitchen where Michael was struggling to fire up the coffee machine. He also seemed to be spilling filter coffee all over François' pristine surfaces.

François barged him out of the way. "Go and sit down. Leave it to me."

Michael sat at the island opposite Darryl. It wouldn't be so bad to keep this gardener around. Michael brought an air of naivety to their lives. One that he and François had long since lost.

"What have you two been discussing?" Michael asked.

"Oh, Darryl was telling me about your plans," François replied.

The machine set off with a decisive gurgle.

Darryl felt such affection for Michael as he reddened.

"He wasn't supposed to see. I wanted to surprise you both with it when it's done."

François sauntered over with a plate of pastries that he plonked down in front of them. "Yes, I figured it was something like that. What a shame you've wasted all that time."

Michael frowned and glanced from François to Darryl.

"Now just wait..." Darryl started.

"Wasted my time? What do you mean?" Michael asked.

"I told you," François said to Darryl. The malice on his face made Darryl ill. "Didn't I say that we should confess to Michael about the car park?"

Michael had gone pale.

"It's just an idea..." Darryl interjected.

"An idea?" François said incredulously. "The bulldozers are booked, and the tarmac is on order. Sorry, Michael, this place will have far too many customers for ornate gardens. Let's face it, I don't think your merry villagers are our target. No, they will come from far and wide when Thorpe Hall reopens. They will need somewhere to leave their Jags and Bentleys."

Michael leapt off his stool. "You're going to turn the gardens into a car park?"

"Not all of them," François said, laying a hand on Michael's arm. "We'll keep the lawns, but let's face it, we only need a groundsman for those. I'm sure you're far too qualified for what will be left over."

"François. Stop it," Darryl shouted.

The betrayal on Michael's face would be etched into Darryl's mind for years to come.

"You've led me on. You pair of bastards."

Chapter Thirteen

Michael stormed out of the kitchen and straight out of the front door. Darryl shuddered as the old oak door slammed behind him. François bit into a pastry as though nothing had happened. Darryl had forgotten just how cold-blooded he could be. "Sometimes you disgust me."

"Oh, for fuck's sake, Darryl. Someone had to put him out of his misery. If it was left to you, he'd be deadheading the rose bushes as they dug around him. It was an act of kindness."

"It was an act of pure venom."

With his appetite for pastries or spending any further time with François severely depleted, he grabbed his coat and went outside. He could see no sign of Michael. Instead, Darryl found himself wandering into the gardens sprawled in front of the old house. He hadn't really taken them in before. With Michael's plans swirling around in his head, he saw that they could be something breath-taking.

A noise had him turning to see François tentatively making his way over. Darryl scowled. "I came out here to have a break from you and your vicious tongue."

"Don't be like that. Come on. You always leave the dirty work to me."

"I mean it, François. There was no need for that. It was cruel."

François kicked an old pebble. "Not as cruel as building his hopes up just so you could fuck him."

Darryl wanted to reply when he realised that François had a point. He had led Michael on, but it wasn't as clear-cut as a need to fuck him. Something about Michael made Darryl want him around.

"You shouldn't be out here anyway," François continued. "You've only just got out of bed. I'm all out of nursing skills if you were planning a relapse."

The suffocation made him want to scream. "You sound like you give a shit."

François put his hand on his shoulder. "I do care. You know I do."

Shrugging him free, Darryl went over to the flower bed that had once held a race car. He'd seen it in the photos before they'd bought the place. He wondered what flowers would bloom here in the spring if they were given half a chance. "We always think we're right, don't we?" he said quietly.

François gave a laugh. "I don't remember us getting it wrong. Burlington Hotels is one of the biggest in the business. That's down to a lot of you and a little of me."

He could turn the charm on when he wanted. Usually, Darryl let François' compliments wash over him, but today they were cloying. "We make money. Is that the only thing we were put on this earth for?"

"Oh Jesus, have you had some kind of epiphany while you were nursing your cold? I'm not sure I can deal with that."

Darryl whirled around. "You'd deal with whatever I threw at you because you're a parasite that adapts."

François looked as though he'd shot him with his harsh words. He swallowed them down and put on a weak smile. "Come on, Darryl. We sleep with someone in every location we open. You've never got all dewy-eyed over them before. We have Kenya soon. Michael will be a distant memory and we'll laugh about this."

François had another point. They had found a night-time distraction in all the locations where Burlington Hotels had a boutique property. Darryl had taken pride in christening each bridal suite they had created. "I need some space. I'm going for a walk. Please don't follow me." He set off down the drive.

"What about the swatches?" François shouted after him.

"You choose. I'm not in the mood."

Storming onto the road, he thought about what must have been going through Michael's head as he'd walked down here only minutes before. Darryl had made it a point not to feel guilt. He'd always thought it an unproductive emotion, but today his body seemed to flow with it.

Once on the main road, he walked towards the village but then stopped. Everyone loved Michael and word spread quickly in a place like Napthwaite. The last thing he fancied were scathing looks and whispered conversations.

Instead, he veered towards the footpath and wandered down to Thorpe Tarn. The day was misty and grey, remarkably like his mood. Bennett's Woods lay silent today. It had felt like a magical land when Michael had shown him the wildlife there. Today it seemed to have closed ranks to this newcomer.

Even the tarn lay empty. The usual heron that had made it home was nowhere to be seen. Darryl perched on an old piece of driftwood and stared across the glassy water.

All his life he had pursued money. A childhood of having no possessions would do that to a person. One Christmas, when he'd been maybe eight or nine, some charitable soul had come to the home dressed as Santa and given out presents. Darryl had been thrilled with his Transformer. It hadn't been one of the sought-after ones, but it was still pretty cool. He'd spent all day changing it from the dinosaur to the robot and back again, pretending that they were going to go on exciting adventures together.

For that afternoon, he'd forgotten about the world that he always thought had abandoned him. But an older kid, Martin Jefferies, hadn't liked his present from Santa. He'd tried to get Darryl to swap, but wild horses wouldn't have made Darryl trade a cool toy for a chess set. It had been his first proper fight.

Darryl rubbed his temple where he could still almost feel Martin's fist connecting, even thirty-odd years later. The bruise of that might have faded, but the feeling in the pit of his stomach when he'd come back from the bathroom to find his toy smashed into pieces would never leave him. He'd cried himself to sleep that night and vowed never to allow anyone take things away from him again.

That same feeling of desolation gnawed at him now. It wasn't that he saw Michael as a plaything. François had been wrong. Michael represented a different life, much the same way as the Transformer had…a life that Darryl could flourish in given half a chance.

At forty-two years old, it was a bit late to be figuring out what he wanted to be when he grew up. Standing, he set off to the Hall. He had created a life that millions would swap theirs for in a heartbeat. He had more money than he knew what to do with, and a knack for making more of it. As he came to the foot of the drive, the Hall reached up to the skies to greet him. It was a beautiful house. Indecision needled at him.

What if this time is different?

Sighing, he made his way inside. François appeared at the door of the study as soon as Darryl came in.

"You've been gone over an hour. I was about to ring the Mountain Rescue."

Hanging his coat up, Darryl grimaced at him. "Which is mostly made up of villagers. The news about our little car park plan has probably spread wider than your legs. I suspect they would leave me to the elements."

François walked over to him. "You're not still in a mood, are you?" He massaged Darryl's shoulders. "I'm sure I could loosen you up."

Darryl lifted François' hands from him, letting them drop. "We only play with others, remember. I don't see anyone else in the room."

François dashed around him. "Perhaps we could make an exception."

Darryl remembered the young Frenchman down on his luck all those years ago. They'd had a brief romance but found they set the board room on fire a lot more than the bedroom. He had a lot to thank François for and in another world, might have taken him up on the offer.

But life had got far too complicated already. Starting a one-on-one love affair with François was most certainly not on the cards.

"Maybe another time, eh?"

Chapter Fourteen

"How you doing?"

James' kind face smiled down at Michael as he lay on the rug by the fireplace. He had spent the whole night thinking about his feelings. It was exhausting.

"I'll be fine. Thank you again. You didn't have to give your flat up. I could have taken one of the guest rooms, you know."

"You're a friend, Michael. You don't have to pay to stay at The King's. Besides, Arthur made us some decent food up at the farm. Even Ed complimented him."

"Did someone say my name?" Arthur crept in closely followed by Will. Michael's stomach dropped.

"What do we have here?" James said, putting his arm around Arthur's waist as he came in for a cuddle. "The gays of Napthwaite Annual General Meeting?"

Will sat down on the rug opposite to Michael and stared hard at him. "Care to tell me what's been going on?"

Michael curled his legs up so his chin rested on his knees. "I did think about coming to you but…"

"But bloody what?"

"You've got enough to deal with."

Will leant forward and slapped Michael on the leg. "Not so much that I'm not here for you."

James sat on the sofa and Arthur perched on his knee. "Seems like you have a queue of friends, Michael."

The three faces staring back at him gave him warmth inside. Adding Ed, Andrew and Hardeep to the equation, not to mention Mrs Turnbull, he had more friends in this small village than he'd ever truly had. It made the decision he'd come to all the more difficult. "I'm very lucky and I appreciate every one of you. However, I think it's time I moved on."

Will sprang back. "Oh great. First Dad leaves me and now you."

"Will, don't," Michael said, reaching out his hand, which Will took. "I can't stay here if I can't earn money."

Will scooted over so he sat next to Michael. "I thought there was a chance Darryl would keep you on. Didn't you say that?"

Michael hadn't really wanted to tell Will yet. Thorpe Hall represented such deep emotion to him. It would be cruel. "That's not going to happen now."

"Come on. Spit it out. If I think you're protecting me again, I'm going to lace your meals with laxatives while you're here."

Michael laughed, despite the overwhelming tension in the room. He looked up at James and Arthur who seemed as eager to find out as Will. "Fine," he sighed. "They're going to tarmac over the gardens to make a car park for their new mega hotel. What's left will be built on with little chalets things and all they're leaving are the lawns, although I bet that's not definite."

James and Arthur looked at each, lost for words. But to Michael's horror, tears filled Will's eyes.

"What? They can't." Will turned to James. "We must be able to stop them. You're the chair of the parish council. Can't you do anything?"

James held his hands up. "They'll have to submit the plans, of course. But as none of it will be seen from the road, I can't really see any grounds to object."

"But...traffic. There'll be an impact on the village. Thorpe Hall is our heritage."

James shook his head. "Burlington Hotels will have that all sewn up. They'll have the best lawyers in the country. It's what they do. Find a content little backwater and turn it into a hotspot."

Will wiped his eyes with his sleeve. "But Dad —"

Michael took hold of his hand. "I shouldn't have told you. I'm sorry."

They sat in silence for a second, letting the full weight of news sink in.

"Those bastards," Arthur exclaimed. James jumped at his ferocity. "Leading you on just to get your kit off. They made out they were the saviours of the whole fucking village the night of the storm."

He couldn't believe that Darryl would be this cruel to him. François perhaps, but not Darryl. He had to be one hell of an actor if he had been making it all up.

"I just don't get it," he told them. "Yesterday morning, Darryl was really into the plans I showed him. He loved having the villagers in the house and he's always on at me to tell him stories about the Hall that your dad shared with me. He even said they could change the use."

"Then what happened?" Will asked, quietly.

"Well, François offloaded their true plan, and I stormed out."

"Fair enough," James said. "They're lucky you didn't knock their blocks off."

"Hang on a minute," Will said, seemingly lost in thought. "That little viper doesn't have a say, and he knows it. He must have seen Darryl dithering and decided to take matters into his own hands."

Michael hadn't thought about conflict between Darryl and François. "What do I do then?" he asked Will.

"You fight," Arthur said, grimly.

As Michael had marched down the drive the night before, he'd made a vow that he would never set foot on the grounds of Thorpe Hall again. "I'm not begging for work," he replied. "François would love that."

"I didn't say beg. I said fight."

James shook his head. "Sounds to me like there's baggage between those two. The last thing you need is to get in between that."

Arthur twisted his ear gently. "That's not what you said when I arrived."

James kissed Arthur. "Fair point. I'm out."

"Arthur's right," Will said. "If Darryl was having second thoughts after seeing a fraction of your plans, then you go and tell him the rest."

Michael threw his head back. "You mean go up there again? Sounds thrilling."

"Not today or tomorrow. Let them stew a bit. Then go up on the proviso that you're collecting your things.

You can discuss your ideas and give it a whirl. You've nothing to lose."

"But..." Michael started.

"François won't allow that," Arthur mused.

"Then we get him out of the way," Will replied.

"Wait a minute," Michael said.

"He never leaves that bloody place. He hates the outdoors," Will said, deep in thought.

"Probably afraid of the rain melting him," Arthur muttered.

"Leave him to me," James said. "He keeps bleating on about getting some decent wine for the Hall while they're up there. I reckon I could get my wholesaler to send some samples up to us in a day or so. He won't be able to resist a free tasting."

Will clapped his hands together making them all jump. "Then we have a plan."

"Do we?" Michael asked. He looked from one to the other, but they all grinned back at him. "Fine. We have a bloody plan."

* * * *

The next two days, Michael could have been a prisoner, albeit in a very swanky cell. He didn't want to bump into François or Darryl and knowing Napthwaite, they would be around every corner.

Instead, he worked his way through James' DVD collection. They were mostly action movies, which wouldn't have been his first choice. By the end of the second day, he didn't know if Bruce Willis had blown up the Death Star or Harrison Ford had been lost in the Matrix. He wished he'd managed to grab some of his books from the Hall before he'd made his grand exit.

"You should open a window in here. It's getting smelly," Will said. He had been feeding Michael as though he were a king, constantly running up the stairs with tasty treats that weren't on the menu downstairs.

Will flung the window open and the cold winter breeze flooded in. Michael hated being hemmed in at the best of times and he'd really missed that freshness.

"Parole day today," Michael said, nibbling on asparagus wrapped in prosciutto.

"Nervous?"

"A bit. I hate doing all the talking. It's not my style."

Will ruffled his hair. "I would hate to put you under pressure by saying the garden that my parents lovingly created on top of many ancestors' land depends on you. So, I'll just say, good luck."

Michael threw the half-eaten asparagus onto the plate. "Cheers."

"I'm joking…a bit."

Will left him to get ready. With most of his clothes still at the Hall, he had done a moonlight raid on his house. Work was very much underway. He'd crept through the building site like a ninja. It seemed strange being home after everything that had happened since he had last been in there. When he'd stood in the lounge, he remembered Matthew coming to see him the night of the storm.

Tears overwhelmed him and he sank down on the window ledge. Although Matthew had sold the Hall fair and square, Michael couldn't shake the feeling he was letting him down. "I will fix this. I promise," he said. He found some jeans and polo shirt. They didn't scream high fashion, but they fitted beautifully.

Once he was satisfied he looked the best he could, he made his way back to The King's. Inside, Becky was lining up wine glasses on a table. She whistled when she saw him walk in. "Now that makes a nice change from combats and an old fleece. You scrub up well."

Michael blushed. "It's nothing. I have no bloody clothes. I'm going up there to get my stuff now."

James walked behind the bar and got him a shot of brandy. He slid it across the bar.

"For luck?"

"Bloody hell, is this a saloon now?" Becky laughed.

Michael knocked it back. The dark brown liquid burned its way down to his belly. It reminded him of that night with François. He had been so loving. "Right, I'd best make myself scarce."

James nodded.

Once out in the open air, Michael turned his collar up and headed off towards Queen Street. Glancing down the road in the direction of the Hall, he saw François marching towards the green.

He'd expected to be angry at seeing his face for the first time, but instead a sadness overtook him. He remembered the time they had shared together when Darryl had been sick. François had given him an insight that couldn't have been faked.

Michael hid behind the big yew tree at the edge of the churchyard and watched. François reached the green and on cue, went straight towards The King's.

James had estimated he could keep François there a couple of hours at best. Michael suspected that would be closer to one hour. François wasn't the type to waste time needlessly.

At the gates of the Hall, he breathed a sigh of relief when he saw Darryl's car parked out front. On his way, he'd panicked that maybe Darryl would take the opportunity to go on some errands. But it stood to reason he would probably luxuriate in a bit of peace.

He banged on the door and ignored the fact that his heartbeat hammered away like some nineties rave tune.

"Where's your key?" Darryl said as he heaved the door open. He stopped in his tracks when he saw who stood on his doorstep. "Michael."

"The very same. I thought I'd get my belongings."

"Oh, of course." Darryl ushered him inside.

"May I?" Michael said, gesturing to the stairs.

"Go for it. Can we speak though? Before you go?"

Michael took a second. Will had told him he didn't have to fill every silence. "Do you think that's a good idea?"

He enjoyed putting it onto Darryl, a trick that Arthur had taught him. It had clearly unsettled Darryl, who must be used to François' histrionics on a daily basis.

"I would like to see if I can make you understand."

Michael set off up the stairs. James had coached him on how body language made all the difference in a negotiation. Walking away from a conversation gave power.

"We'll probably need a drink for that," he said over his shoulder.

"I'll be waiting in the study."

It took every bit of strength he had not to run across the landing and into his room, the same way he had after the first night he had slept with Darryl and François. With shaking hands, he stuffed his belongings into bags.

He wouldn't get it all to The King's in one go, but if things went really tits up, he had an army of volunteers who would do the honours.

Mindful that François would be home soon, Michael roughly piled the bags onto the bed and made his way onto the landing. He crept down the stairs and listened at the study door. He couldn't hear anything. He thought about all the training that his friends had given him, swallowed hard and opened the door.

Chapter Fifteen

Darryl sat in one chair, but it didn't look natural. Then he sat in the other but didn't like his back to the door. Next, he tried standing by the fireplace, but looked like someone from *Downton Abbey*. He hadn't been this nervous in years.

As he heard Michael trying to be quiet coming down the stairs but creaking every step, he threw himself on the sofa. Grabbing François' copy of *The Hotelier*, he found himself reading an article on the next big thing in dishwashers, as the door opened.

To his amazement, his body felt alive with tension. It had been quite some time since a man had made Darryl Burlington feel like this.

Michael walked through the door. He also looked pretty terrified, which Darryl found endearing. The men he usually bedded were confident and always tried to match him. They wanted the billionaire to see them as a challenge and stick around. But Michael seemed to be different. That made the guilt at what he and François had done to him all the harder to take.

"All packed?" Darryl said with forced cheerfulness.

Michael nodded and came to stand by the fire. François had left it banked up because Darryl never remembered to keep it going.

"Andrew said he would come with his van tomorrow," Michael said. "If that's all right?"

Darryl put the magazine to his side on the sofa. "Of course. Just message François."

Michael dithered which intrigued Darryl.

"Is there something else?" Darryl asked.

He hated being cold like this. Every instinct inside him told him to grab hold of Michael and beg his forgiveness, but he suspected that would be the worst thing he could do right now.

Michael sighed and fiddled with a candlestick on the mantelpiece. "I just wanted to say that I appreciate the help you gave me. I'm sorry I stormed out the other day but—"

"Michael, it's me who should apologise. Actually no. It's fucking François who should be the one to say sorry. One day his pointed little tongue is going to get him in trouble that I won't be able to bail him out of."

A flash of amusement appeared on Michael's face. "But you did trick me," he said. "François was right about that, wasn't he?"

Darryl crossed his legs. "Trick is a strong word. Nothing is decided for this place yet. It's true, the plan is to turn it into a destination hotel."

Michael ran his hand through his hair. "Don't you care about the history? What it could be with some tender care?"

His earnest face did nothing for the guilt swishing around Darryl's gut.

"Michael, listen to me. I'm a billionaire, it's true. I made that money by finding gems like Thorpe Hall. I founded Burlington Hotels on that skill. But I am not Burlington Hotels. I have a board and investors. How do you think they would react if I just bought the Hall from them?"

Michael frowned. "Why would they care? I'm sure there are other buildings on your list that can make them even more money."

"They would stop trusting me if it got out that I bought this place because I was in lust with the gardener. Their money would disappear quicker than free pints in The King's. They invest in me as well as the company."

"So that's it then?"

Darryl shook his head. "I told you. It's all up in the air. François has booked the workmen."

"Can I email you my final plans?" Michael asked, hopefully.

He knew he should put this beautiful man out of his misery, but Darryl couldn't face the door slamming shut. "It can't hurt," he said with his best winning smile.

"Is this just a joke to you? People think very highly of this Hall. Never mind the impact you will have on the village if you build this monstrosity. Napthwaite is special and you think you can make it into Benidorm."

Darryl got off the sofa and took hold of Michael's arm. "Hey, I'm sorry. I didn't mean to come across as blasé about it." He reached up and put his hand on Michael's chest. "Calm down," Darryl soothed.

"I'm perfectly calm, thank you." Michael reached up to remove Darryl's hand but instead rested it on top.

"I've missed you," Darryl murmured.

Swallowing hard, Michael made no effort to move away. Their lips were almost touching. Michael's breath washed over his face.

"This is a bad idea," Michael whispered.

"The best kind," Darryl murmured, before locking lips with him.

At first their lips just grazed each other. Michael squeezed Darryl's hand, giving him all the encouragement he needed.

He pressed his lips ever so slightly harder against Michael's. His heart leapt with joy when Michael returned the kiss. He had missed Michael so much in the last few days. More than he would care to admit. With his free hand, he grabbed hold of Michael's waist and pulled him toward him, his chest imprisoning their clasped hands.

The kiss became more frantic. Michael reached up and ran his hands over the back of Darryl's head, the contact making his cock swell.

Overwhelmed by his feelings, he pushed his tongue into Michael's mouth. Freeing his hand, he wrapped it around Darryl's shoulder. He wanted to explore that naked body so much.

In sync, they dropped down onto the floor, Michael lying on top of Darryl and grinding his cock into his body. Darryl ran both hands through Michael's hair, wrapping his legs around him. His need for this man was all-consuming.

Straddling him, Michael flung open his shirt. The air hit Darryl's body at the same time as Michael's mouth. Michael kissed, licked and bit his nipples. Darryl cried out in joy.

Michael dragged his own top off and threw it on the sofa. Leaning down to kiss him again, Darryl loved his hairy chest brushing against his own.

Spinning them over so Michael was on his back, Darryl shrugged his shirt off. He ran his hands across Michael's perfect body. He followed the hairline from his chest, down his torso to his waistband. Anticipation flooded his system. Flipping the buttons on the trousers, he dived his hand inside. Michael's rock-solid cock had already started leaking pre-cum. Darryl rubbed the head with his thumb before bringing it out and licking it. "You taste amazing."

Michael dragged his jeans and underwear down. His thick cock lay waiting for attention. "Show me how much you like it," Michael whispered.

Darryl kicked his shoes off before losing his own jeans and boxers. His cock yearned for attention that he needed it to be free.

Crouching to the side of Michael, he gripped his cock by the base and hungrily enveloped him with his mouth. There would be no teasing today — his need was almost too much.

Michael responded to the pace, bucking his hips, cajoling Darryl to take him all in. Darryl sucked hard. God, it felt good. He pulled away, wiping his mouth. "Fuck, you are so sexy," he murmured.

Sitting up, Michael kissed him. At the same time, he reached down and wrapped his fingers around Darryl's cock. Darryl thought he might come immediately, but Michael knew what he was doing.

Michael kicked one of his legs out of his trousers and underwear before straddling his chest, his beautiful cock only centimetres away. Michael stared down at him.

Darryl took his cock in his mouth again and grabbed hold of both his hips, moving them in time. Using the sofa behind them as support, Michael took over the momentum, fucking Darryl's mouth. His full balls slapping on Darryl's chin. His own were desperate for release. Reaching down, he took hold of his cock with his right hand whilst gripping Michael's solid butt cheek with his left.

"Oh, fuck yeah," Michael grunted.

Darryl prepared himself. He needed this so badly. Michael didn't disappoint. With a final cry, he drove his cock deep into Darryl's mouth. Hot cum filled Darryl's mouth.

The sensory overload was too much for Darryl. Still sucking on Michael's spent cock, Darryl pulled at his own dick until his orgasm exploded in his hand. He let Michael's cock drop as he arched his neck, groaning.

Darryl didn't move for a second. The aftershocks were too delicious to disturb.

Suddenly the room lit up by the security lights on the drive.

"Shit, François is home," Darryl exclaimed.

Michael leapt off him and they struggled with their clothes. Once they had managed to get them on, Darryl cringing as he hadn't even had time to clean himself up, they stood by the fire.

"Are you ashamed?" Michael said eventually.

Darryl kissed him. "Of course not. But I've had enough grief for the time being."

François came in the room. He looked shocked when he saw Michael standing on the hearth rug as though nothing had happened. "Oh, hello. I didn't expect to find you here."

"I'm full of surprises," Michael replied.

"Aren't you just?"

François came into the room and sat on the sofa…in the exact spot Michael had been fucking Darryl's mouth only minutes before.

"Well, I'll certainly have a look at that email," Darryl said.

"What email?" François asked with a scowl. "You don't even know your password."

"Michael is going to send the plans anyway. It can't hurt, can it?"

François sighed. "Whatever. I've had an hour of drinking vinegar at the local hostelry. All I can think about now is a bath and a decent glass of wine."

"I'll see myself out then," Michael said.

"That's good of you," François muttered, kicking his boots off and rubbing his feet.

Michael stopped at the door and looked at Darryl. "Think about what I said. A lot of people care about this Hall. Napthwaite isn't a place to be underestimated."

Chapter Sixteen

François let the book slide off his chest onto the floor and stared up at the ceiling. Seeing Michael in the study last night had made him happy and threatened all at the same time. Darryl had just shrugged when François had attempted to interrogate him as to what he'd wanted. Deep down he might like Michael, but François didn't trust him. Anyone would think this gloomy old house was Buckingham bloody Palace.

He had never seen Darryl behave like this before. Usually, they went straight into developing a hotel, but he was dragging his heels on this one. François had workmen provisionally booked in, but Darryl had changed the start date three times now. The hypnotic powers of Michael's cock were very impressive.

The radio went on in the kitchen, which meant the lord of this manor was up. François padded through to the kitchen where he found Darryl pottering around. He watched his abortive effort at working out the coffee machine for a few seconds before nudging him out of the way. "Let me do it. Am I the only person who can work this damned thing?"

"You always complain I don't do anything. You won't bloody let me," Darryl replied.

The atmosphere Michael had left between them clearly hadn't dissipated in the night. François could not face another day of being punished for a tiny outburst. "Okay, Darryl. What is the issue? You've been like a bear with a sore head."

Darryl faced him. "Fine. I didn't like the way you spoke to Michael last night."

He tried his best to hide his annoyance at this revelation. *Fucking Michael again.* "Then I will apologise," he said. "You have it bad for this one."

"There you go again. You sound like a jealous child."

His feelings were giving him away. "I'm not jealous of him, but I think he read too much into our…arrangement. Now he stands to get hurt. That's not a good situation to be in. For any of us."

"What do you think he meant when he said Napthwaite shouldn't be underestimated?"

"Oh, fuck knows," François said, a little too aggressively. "These people never leave this bloody place. I'm surprised they don't still have rationing."

Darryl sat at the table and put his head in his hands. "He could do us real damage. What if he turns the whole bloody village on us?"

François finally fired the coffee machine into life and sat opposite him.

"And what difference will that make? We have staff. We have suppliers. They can do what they like. You don't really care what they think, do you? Jesus, Darryl. We've had to deal with worse than this. Remember that residents' committee in Barcelona? Or how about the guardians of those bloody turtles in Sardinia? Now you're shitting yourself that Mrs Turnbull will give you the cold shoulder in Poole's emporium of inedible food? I'm sure survival will not be beyond us."

Darryl rubbed his eyes. "Don't you ever get bored? For the last eight years we've done the same thing over and over. Find a location, develop it, move on."

François took hold of his hand. "That is what we excel at. I can't quite see you giving it up to grow vegetables."

"Would you help me dig them up if I did?"

"I might. If the pay was right."

Darryl squeezed François' hand. "We've been through a lot, you and me. You've always had my back. I do appreciate that, you know."

François' stomach fluttered like a teenager's. Compliments were few and far between from Darryl. When they did appear, they were like rainbows.

"I am here to talk sense into you when a hard body distracts you. It's part of my job description."

Darryl grinned. "It is very distracting, isn't it?"

François nodded. Michael's body had filled a lot of his thoughts since they'd arrived in Napthwaite.

"Maybe I was just in a sex haze last night," Darryl continued.

"Did you?"

"Just a little."

François dropped his hand. "You are incorrigible."

Darryl grabbed his hand again, a glint in his eye. "Don't tell me you didn't while I was ill."

François tried to free his hand. "I might have done. There was nothing on the television."

"It's so bloody confusing," Darryl said, finally releasing his hand. "It's like you bring out the best in one half of me. Without you, I'd be shit at all this. But with Michael, I don't feel in charge. He doesn't want anything from me. I like it."

Typical Darryl to put himself firmly in the centre of everything.

"Sounds like you're looking to settle down," François said. He couldn't ignore the glimmer of hope that he could be the person Darryl would do that with. However, he had to admit that Michael fitted that role far better.

"I'm not looking for anything. I should stick to what I have and be grateful."

It didn't sound very convincing. Alarm flooded François' system. "Now we've settled that, I've got the first images from Kenya. There are about thirty places we need to narrow down. That might perk you up."

"See, I need you as a slave driver." Darryl got up. "Is there a coffee incoming anytime soon?"

"The milk is on the turn. I'd better nip into the village to get some more. You make a start on the files — they're in the main folder. If I'm not back in half an hour, call the police. Mrs Turnbull could be holding me against my will in Poole's storeroom. Mind you, if they force half of that crap in my mouth, I'd give them all your secrets." Without waiting for an answer, François went out in the hallway and threw his coat on. Rage swirled around in him. *Who the fuck is this gardener to try to fuck up what we have? I haven't pushed that man to the top of his game for it to be ruined.*

He ruminated over his next move as he made his way up the road towards the green. He would be glad when their time in this bloody village was a memory.

The King's Arms stood proudly facing the church as it had done for hundreds of years. François had thought it a charming pub before. Now he saw it as the headquarters of his enemy. Darryl had let slip that that was where Michael had holed up, and François knew exactly what to do.

As he entered the bar, James' face hardened. Of course, they would all be on the side of the poor handsome gardener mercilessly tricked into bed by the two strangers in their midst.

"I'd like to speak to Michael," François said. "If you would be so kind."

"Who says he's here?" James answered.

François didn't even grace that pathetic attempt at subterfuge with a response. Instead, he sighed loudly and glanced at his watch.

James blinked first and walked over to the door that had a sign reading *Rooms upstairs* above it.

"Michael. You've a visitor." He let the door bang. "If you'd care to take a seat, Mr Fleming will be right with you. Could I sell you a drink while you wait? This being a pub."

François threw his scarf and jacket down onto the seat. "I won't be risking a glass of wine, that is for sure. I'll take an ale."

"Half?" James asked.

"A pint. Make that two. Civility doesn't have to have a high price."

James smiled sweetly and headed off to the bar to prepare the drinks. A few locals sat at the bar and scowled across at him. They were so stereotypical that François almost laughed in their faces. It would be good to finally be in London again where no one knew your business. How bored were these people?

Michael came through the door. François cursed himself as the butterflies swirled through him.

This is just lust, Vernier. Stay focused.

"Michael. Won't you join me?"

He gestured to the seat opposite him. Michael dithered, the uncertainty making François strangely proud of his effect on him.

"Is that a good idea?"

"I've ordered you a pint. At least drink it with me. I won't bite you in front of these good people."

Michael sighed and came over, sitting his muscular frame into the chair. François remembered the weight of that body and his cock twitched in response. "How have you been?" he said.

A memory of watching Darryl and Michael fuck flashed into his mind. He would be fighting a full-blown erection at this rate.

Thankfully James brought two terribly poured pints over. François winced when he saw the beer dripping down the side and waterlogging the beer mats on the table. Once James was out of range, François produced a tissue from his pocket and made the glass drinkable. "All his life behind that bar and this is the best he can do?" he muttered. Satisfied that the glass wouldn't cover him in beer, he raised it.

"Here's to the future."

Michael didn't return his salutation. Instead, he picked the glass up and took a long swig. François matched him, taking a big gulp. He hated to admit but they did stock good beer in The King's. He had been keen to get the same supplier for the Hall, but they could forget it.

"Now we've done all the necessary messing around. I've a feeling you've come here to say something so it's probably best you get it out," Michael said.

Michael seemed to have been taking lessons in how to handle himself. "Direct. I like that. I'm here for you really."

Michael nodded. "Is that right?"

"Yes. I heard all about your…visit last night. Michael, listen. Darryl is a complicated man. He had a horrendous upbringing and overcame such a lot. But it left terrible scars. I've known him for eight years and I understand him. This whim of his is exactly that. A whim. He will be onto the next shiny prize before you know it."

Michael took another swig of his drink. "Let me guess. You think I should cease all contact with him and disappear like a good boy?"

"Of course not. Come and see us whenever you like while we're here. You'll get a warm welcome from both of us. I can guarantee that."

"Or either of you, if my memory serves."

François shrugged. "Or either. If you want both, better to make an appointment. It doesn't do to leave these things to chance. Once we start ripping the place to pieces, there won't be enough hours in the day."

"Why are you being like this?"

"Like what?"

"This isn't the published poet who I made love with all that weekend."

François hadn't been expecting that and it winded him. He had come fully prepared to fight for Darryl but to fight the person Michael thought he was had not been on the agenda.

"I'm many things to many people, Michael."

"I don't believe that."

François took a gulp of his pint for no other reason than to buy some time.

"Know what I do believe?" Michael continued, unperturbed.

"Illuminate me."

"I believe you revealed more to me than you meant to. I believe you see me as a threat to your relationship with Darryl. And I believe you to be better than this acid queen role you've adopted."

To François' horror, tears pricked his eyes. Michael would not do this to him and certainly not in the local pub. Slowly he placed his pint down on the table. "I showed you what I chose to because I knew a sap like you would throw his knickers on my bedpost straight after. As for you being a threat? Darryl won't even remember your name this time next year. My apologies if you see a friendly drink as being acidic. I'm simply being neighbourly. You're no more a rival to me than Liz Poole is to Angelina Jolie. But like I said, I like you. Seeing you get hurt is not on my agenda."

François didn't know if his reply had hit home, but his work here was done now. He only wanted Michael to know that he could fight hard. Never let it be said that François Vernier didn't give his enemies fair warning.

He got up and started to put his coat and scarf on. "I should really be on the move. We've got so many potential properties for the next project. Kenya. So exciting. I wonder who will be waiting for us there."

He produced a ten-pound note from his pocket and threw it down on the bar.

"Keep the change."

"Too kind," James replied.

As he walked towards the door, Michael blocked his path. François hoped he wasn't going to cause a scene. "Are you going to bar me from leaving?"

"You are wrong on so many levels, François. I will not let you destroy that garden."

"Thorpe Hall Hotel and Conferencing Centre will be opening on schedule. On private land, I might add. Don't make a fool of yourself. Now get out of my way."

Michael stood to one side, and François pushed the door open.

The cold air hit him, and he turned, relishing in the fact that Michael, James and the grim locals were all staring at him.

"To show there's no hard feelings, how about you give me a list of any cuttings you want, and I'll do my best to pull some up for you? Be quick though. The bulldozers are booked."

Chapter Seventeen

"He's a jumped-up little shitbag."

"I know but—"

"No buts. How fucking dare he speak to you like that?"

Will took a decisive sip of his wine and glowered. Andrew and Hardeep shifted uncomfortably. All eyes were on Michael as if he were somehow responsible for François' hostile behaviour. The remains of a Sunday roast lay before them, two hopeful dogs doing circuits of the table.

Hardeep put his hand on Will's arm. "Calm yourself. It's not Michael's fault. He's done his best."

Will's face relaxed. "I'm sorry, Michael. That came out wrong. I just feel responsible. It was my idea to sell the bloody place. All of this is my fault."

Michael knew Will had tortured himself over that decision every day since the storms.

"I can't believe he can change like this," Michael said. "If you saw the François I did, you'd be the same. Deep down there is a different person in there."

Andrew shook his head. "That's the same for anyone. Anger and aggression hide fear usually. He must have issues."

"Boo fucking hoo," Will added.

Hardeep cleared the plates. Michael leapt to attention to help. "Another amazing meal, Will. Thank you."

"Not at all. I'm sorry I've bent your ear the whole time."

Andrew stood. "I'm going to have to love you and leave you all. It's parish council night. I can hardly wait to hear Mrs Turnbull's presentation on the plants for the village summer display."

Will seemed lost in thought. "Can't you raise about the Hall at the meeting? There must be something they can do. What's the bloody point of it otherwise?"

"There have been no planning applications yet. I doubt we will get much of a say anyway. It will go straight to County." Letting the other two finish cleaning. Will got up and got his coat off the hook.

"What are you doing?" Andrew asked.

Michael froze. Will had that look on his face again.

"Coming with you. Public are allowed to address the council, aren't they? I want them to know what's happening." Will announced. He looked ready for battle.

Andrew seemed lost for words for a second.

"I will go," Michael said.

They all turned to him.

"It's my responsibility and I can tell them exactly what I know."

Andrew visibly relaxed. "You need to calm down," he said to Will. "I have just the thing for that."

Will looked unsure.

"Washing up. Hardeep can wash and you can dry. Hours of fun."

Hardeep handed Will the pile of plates.

"But I bloody cooked it."

"Life's a bitch." Hardeep kissed him on the lips. "But we'll be together. What more could you ask for?"

Clearly knowing when he was beaten, Will accepted the plates.

"Fine but leave nothing out," he said to Michael. "Well, perhaps don't tell them everything. Mrs Turnbull doesn't need to know about you being spit roasted every chance you got."

"Hark at Miss Prim over there," Andrew said.

"I mean it. You don't want the council thinking this is just sour grapes from a spurned lover. I know James knows the truth, but the others need to think you're doing this for Napthwaite."

After his dismal performance against François at The King's, Michael had a suspicion they didn't think he was up to this fight.

"You ready?" Andrew asked, putting on his coat.

"I hate leaving you with all this work," Michael said.

Will stuck his head through the kitchen doorway. "Go forth and fight, Fleming. That is all we ask of you."

Shaking his head, he went to get his coat. He saw Andrew and Hardeep mutter something to each other before exchanging a kiss.

"I'll see you later," Andrew called to Will who dashed through and planted a kiss on his lips.

"See you later."

Michael averted his eyes. Sometimes these three forgot there were other people in the room. It made him uncomfortable and jealous in equal measures.

They set off down the lane, leaving Hardeep to calm Will down.

"I'm worried about him," Andrew said.

Michael agreed. Will's behaviour was concerning him too. But they didn't need a fourth member of their group.

"He's getting obsessed with the Hall. I can understand why, but I feel I'm letting him down."

Andrew patted him on the shoulder. "Don't be ridiculous. Will doesn't see you as the bad guy. He thinks if they hadn't sold the place, his father would still be alive."

"I get that but if I'd been a bit more professional instead of falling into bed with them. I might have held more sway."

Andrew chuckled. "I always find that putting a man's cock in your mouth gives you a certain degree of influence."

Michael thought about both men's cocks in his mouth. Even after François coming in all guns blazing, he still had moments at night where he thought about the times they had shared. He wished he could compartmentalise like they did.

Andrew looked at him in the moonlight. "You still like them, don't you?"

"Is it that obvious?"

"I'm afraid so, my friend. You're too good for this world, Michael. Honestly you are."

They carried on across the green and up Queen Street towards the village hall.

"I hope they've finally sorted the heating out," Andrew said. "It was bloody freezing last time."

As they went in, the rest of the council were already there. Christine Carrington sat next to James, chatting about something Arthur had told her at work. Mrs Turnbull seemed to be telling Rob Holdsworth a long story about her latest bake sale being held that weekend. Even Liz Poole sat in the corner. Michael sat next to her in the public seats.

"Hello, Liz," he said.

He still didn't trust her after the debacle in the summer where she'd tried to get Arthur sacked. James insisted they had moved on, but Michael knew trouble when he saw it.

"Hello, Michael. Fancy seeing you here."

"I could say the same."

"We're sponsoring Mrs T's bloody flowers this year. Every shop takes its turn. Money thrown down the pan if you ask me, but anything for a quiet life."

Andrew took his seat. Everyone around that table had impacted Michael's life in a different way in the last year. He loved this village and a determination burned in his belly.

"How about you?" Liz asked.

Just as he started to answer, James cleared his throat. The meeting had begun.

Michael hadn't realised quite how boring these sessions were. He'd only heard about the confrontations that sounded like something from reality television.

Eventually, after a long discussion on lupins versus hollyhocks, Mrs Turnbull sat down.

"Do we have any business from the public seats?" James asked.

Nerves jangling, Michael stood.

"Thank you for this opportunity. I'm a man of few words so I'll try to keep it brief. I've come about Thorpe Hall."

A murmur rippled across the table. Michael walked over to them.

"As you all know, Burlington Hotels are going to open it as a hotel. I don't think the village know what this will mean. The impact it will have on us all."

"More people, more customers," Liz piped up.

"Mrs Poole, if you could let Mr Fleming speak," James said.

Liz scowled at her brother but said nothing more.

"They are going to make major changes to the site. Of course, they can't touch the outside of the Hall itself. That's listed. But they have plans to build on it as well as create lodge accommodation on the lawns."

He suddenly realised it had all gone quiet in the room. He had their attention. "I haven't seen the plans as such, but they have told me that they intend to destroy the two-hundred-year-old gardens by creating a car park."

"Oh, my," Mrs Turnbull said, clutching at her pussy bow collar. "Matthew loved those gardens."

"As for the idea that it will bring more customers," Michael continued, getting into his flow, "I think that's a false impression. They have suppliers for everything, and their business model is that the guest never needs to leave the site."

"No doubt they will be traipsing all over the hills though," Rob said. "Leaving litter and needing rescuing the first sign of bad weather."

"The increased traffic will have an impact too," Christine added.

Liz stood up. "Am I right in thinking they are going to take over our village and rinse it for all the cash they can?"

"Mrs Poole," James insisted. "I won't tell you again."

This time Liz wouldn't be swayed and looked at Michael from across the heads of the people sat at the table.

"I'm afraid so," he replied.

"But they'll destroy Napthwaite," Mrs Turnbull exclaimed.

"No, they bloody well won't," Liz said. "Because we won't let them."

"I give up," James said. "If there are any councillors who would like to contribute, I would be most grateful."

"I have lived in this village all my life," Mrs Turnbull said. She wiped her eye with a tissue from up her sleeve before continuing. "I have seen more changes than you give me credit for, but common decency has always been there. Very well hidden sometimes, but always there."

She threw a glare at Liz who pointedly ignored her barb. "I will not let this, this, this *southerner* take our way of life," she continued. "Who's with me?"

The room was silent. Mrs Turnbull gathered herself and wiped her eye. It had been quite the rousing speech.

But it didn't look like anyone else was going to join her. Michael looked at Andrew pleadingly. Before he could do anything, Rob Holdsworth raised his hand. "I'm with you."

Christine followed his lead. "So am I."

Andrew and James looked to each other, then shrugged and raised their hands.

"That's unanimous then," James said. "Napthwaite will not take this lying down."

They all cheered.

* * * *

"Mrs Turnbull channelling Emmeline Pankhurst? Now that I would like to see."

Will and Michael were leaning on a gate, watching the rugby team practice. They were pretending to support a very muddy Andrew. In reality they were checking out all the other men who lived in Napthwaite.

"James has great legs though, doesn't he?" Will continued.

"Will!" Michael exclaimed.

"What? I've got more than my fair share at home, I realise. But it doesn't hurt to appraise the field."

Michael shook his head. "It's good to see you smile."

Will faced Michael. "I feel like a weight's been lifted from my shoulders now I know the village are behind us. Andrew said they were all fired up after the meeting."

"They were, but don't get your hopes up. Darryl Burlington is worth a lot of money. His legal people will tie us in knots."

"There's more than one way to skin a cat, you know. I know he thinks his guests won't need anything, but we can be a pretty unforgiving village when we want to be."

"It's not the guests' fault."

"Collateral damage." Will sniffed.

"The gardens will be gone by then anyway."

"True, but let me have my revenge fantasy."

The whistle went on the pitch and the filthy men made their way to the changing rooms. Rob Holdsworth jogged over.

"If I catch you perving over my squad again, I'll have you cleaning the boots."

Will stuck out his tongue. "You're just not used to actual spectators. Who is your next match against? Happy Days Retirement Home?"

Rob shook his head. "That was a silly charity thing. Andrew tells you way too much."

"You'd be surprised."

"I wouldn't. How are you, Michael? Recovered from Mrs Turnbull's rousing speech?"

"Getting there," Michael said.

"I think she's brilliant," Will added. "I've been telling everyone how my dad would hate what those bastards are going to do to the Hall. I reckon I can get the local paper to cover us too."

"Because that turned out so well last time," Michael said.

When Andrew had been standing for the parish council, Will had arranged for an interview. Andrew's violent ex had traced his location through it and attacked him.

"Fucking hell. It's been quite a year when you think about it. And they say nothing happens in the country," Rob said.

"Right, I need to get to work," Will said. "Walk with me?"

He and Michael said their goodbyes to Rob and set off towards The King's.

"Will, can I ask you something?"

"Of course."

Andrew's words the other night kept reverberating around in Michael's head and he needed to speak to Will. "I know you're angry about the Hall. Believe me,

I share that. But you're not going over the top to deflect your real feelings, are you?"

Will stopped in his tracks. "Meaning?"

"You said yourself you have guilt about your dad selling up. Would you have cared the same if you were still in London?"

He'd gone too far and instantly regretted his words.

"Whether I have guilt about Dad selling or about all the years I spent in London is my affair, Michael. I appreciate that you're getting brave with Darryl and François, but what I don't appreciate is amateur psychoanalysis. If I want professional help, I will seek it out."

Michael watched Will march across the green.

Why do I always put my foot in it?

Chapter Eighteen

Darryl sighed loudly. François glanced up from his laptop to see him looking irritated, an expression that was wearingly common these days.

"I see grumpy Darryl is back in residence. What's up now?"

"I'm bloody sick of these now. After a while, a once-in-a-lifetime safari opportunity is like the previous once-in-a-lifetime safari opportunity."

They had been reviewing potential properties in Kenya all day. Even François had seen enough.

"Maybe we should choose the crockery patterns for this place then, for a change. They sent some great designs through."

Darryl slammed the lid shut on his laptop. The afternoon was melting into dusk. He flicked the lamp on and stood up, stretching. "I'm done for the day."

François shut the lid on his machine too. No doubt Darryl would require some form of entertainment for the evening. "Shall I make us some food?"

At the window, Darryl stared out at the grey skies. "I'm going stir crazy in here. Let's go out for dinner."

François threw another log on the fire. "And where do you suggest? The top-class French restaurant or maybe the sushi place?"

Darryl turned. "I know you hate it here."

"Hate is a strong word. We don't fit in, let's be honest."

Sitting on the window ledge, Darryl ran his hand over his face. "Well, another month or so and we can see what Mombasa has to offer. This place will be well under way. We can leave it to Stan to do the heavy lifting."

François shuddered. His nemesis, Stan Davies, the UK operations project manager. He had come close to losing his voice through shouting at Stan the last time they had worked together. He had no expectations this time would be any different.

"Don't pull that face," Darryl laughed. "He gets it done."

"Eventually," François added.

"Come on, let's go to The King's. I'm sure they've forgotten your performance by now."

François wasn't so sure about that. He'd confessed everything to Darryl when he'd got back and received a stern telling off for his trouble. "I don't think that's a very good idea, do you?"

"How about I buy you an ice cream if you promise to keep your nasty little mouth under control?"

François scowled at him. "Don't start on your high horse. I simply tried to make things a little cleaner for everyone concerned."

"Which backfired as usual. If we go for dinner, it's the perfect opportunity for you to mend some bridges.

I told you the other night, it will make the hotel's success that much easier if the locals are on side."

François couldn't care less. Mentally he had already checked out of this backwater. "You're paying though. I refuse to squander my hard earned on that muck."

"Come on, misery guts. Even you said the food there was decent."

"I say a lot of things I don't mean."

"Now that I won't argue with."

"Like when I told you those trousers suited you."

Darryl whirled around. "You said my ass looked like a peach in these."

"See. I'm so convincing."

They threw their coats on and wandered into the village. As usual absolutely nothing was going on. François wondered how these people survived. Every day must be the same. No wonder they had all panicked when the electricity went. They'd had to examine the futility of their lives instead of watching television. Poor souls.

The King's was doing a roaring trade. Most tables were occupied. James was doing his best to keep the queue at the bar down while Becky whizzed from one table to the next, taking orders and delivering food.

"Blimey, what time is it?" Darryl asked.

"It's only seven."

James' face changed from menial host to scowling sentry the minute he saw Darryl and François. "How can I help?"

"Hi, James. We were wondering if you had a table."

"No, sorry."

Darryl looked taken aback for a second. "I haven't even told you when for yet."

"No need," James said. His expression still one of total revulsion. "I don't have a table for you."

François' ears pricked up. Michael had brought in the troops, had he? This was an unexpected move from Mr Perfect. François could almost respect him.

"Perhaps we'll just stay for a drink then," Darryl said.

"We don't like standing drinkers," James said, wilfully ignoring the three men propping up the bar. They laughed amongst themselves, clearly enjoying their discomfort.

"Let's leave it," François said. "I can make us something infinitely more palatable than this slop."

If François thought he could get a rise out of James, he thought wrong. James just returned that ridiculously fake smile and waited for them to clear the bar.

Half-dragging him, François manoeuvred Darryl outside the pub.

"What the fuck?" Darryl said.

"Come on, let's go to Poole's. It will probably be an impossible mission but if I can find at least three edible items, I'll cook."

They wandered across the green, but the concern on Darryl's face wasn't going anywhere. "This is your frigging fault. You had to come over all Alexis Colby in the pub and now they're closing ranks. What did I tell you about small communities?"

"Relax. It's Stan's issue now. He's as thick as they are. I've no doubt he'll talk them around. I can just see him and Mrs Turnbull mooning over the garden wall at each other."

Darryl shook his head. François stole a glance and did not like what he saw. For some reason this village had got under Darryl's skin. He steeled himself for going into the convenience store. It should be against trade descriptions to call itself that.

They browsed the aisles and François managed to find some chicken that wasn't grey and some vegetables that hadn't shrivelled. A minor feat, judging by his previous attempts at shopping here.

Two villagers roughly pushed past him, almost knocking him into the courgettes.

"Do you mind?"

They ignored him. Darryl didn't though.

"Will they be chasing us out of town with pitchforks soon?"

François scowled and took his basket to Liz at the counter.

She rang them up on the till. "Fifteen pounds, please."

"Fifteen pounds for two manky bits of chicken and some courgettes? Are you joking?"

Darryl huffed behind him.

Liz waited for him to pay. François would not be taken for a fool.

"That chicken is three pounds fifty and the courgettes are one fifty. I think you're ten pounds out. A simple mistake, I'm sure…for some."

"The ten is for insurance. Word on the street is your money isn't good. If I put a tenner in the Mountain Rescue collection, the village will forgive me."

François glanced at Darryl. "This is outrageous."

Darryl pushed past him and slammed a twenty-pound note down on the counter. "Put it all in the Mountain Rescue and we'll bid you good day."

This time he dragged François out of the shop.

"That rotten, greasy-haired shrew," François exclaimed. "How dare she? Is that even legal? I've a good mind to ring the police on her."

"Come on," Darryl said roughly. "It's like there are eyes in every window." He set a rapid pace toward the Hall that François struggled to keep up with.

He knew he had caused this, and it would absolutely fall on him to fix it. "I don't know why you're getting yourself in a stew. These nobodies won't be able to change anything."

As they were crossing a bridge, Darryl whirled around. The look of abject rage on his face made François scared. "It may be an alien concept to you, but I don't like hurting people. We are upsetting everyone in this village, François."

"What do you want to do? Cancel the project?"

"Don't be ridiculous. I think we should probably keep a low profile."

"Amen to that."

When they got to the Hall, François set about cooking their meal. Darryl went into the study to check his emails.

"I don't fucking believe this," Darryl shouted.

François screwed his eyes shut. Nothing good ever came from that statement.

The door banged open, and Darryl stood there like an extra from a Western movie.

"What now?"

"The cleaners have cancelled. They say they're too busy to carry on."

"Then I'll find us some more tomorrow. You're hardly going to expire if you have to put a cup in the dishwasher."

Darryl yanked out a chair at the table and sat down. "First the pub, then the shop and now the cleaners. Your behaviour is ruining us before we've even begun. You need to fix this."

* * * *

Once Darryl had been fed and settled, playing some stupid racing game on his computer, François quietly let himself out of the house. He had been mulling over this plan the whole time he had been cooking. It was his zen time and most of his schemes came up in the kitchen.

Big drops of rain ran down his back. Did it ever stop raining in this place? For once he thanked his lucky stars Queen Street lay deserted. For what he had in mind, he didn't need any witnesses. Standing outside the door to Poole's, he wondered how he had got so unlucky that he had to visit this dump twice in a day.

Putting on his best game face, he walked into the shop. Liz occupied her stoop as usual, and her body straightened when he came in.

"You can't keep away," she said. "What can I get you?"

"There is nothing I want in here," François replied. "Except five minutes of your time."

She seemed intrigued. A good sign. "The coast is clear. I suppose I can give you that."

François had practiced this speech in his head ever since Darryl had told him off. "I hoped to get some advice from you. As a woman at the heart of the community, would you be so kind as to tell me why the locals appear to have taken against us?"

Liz leaned forward on the counter. François caught a whiff of her supermarket perfume and tried his best not to wrinkle his nose.

"Smashing up the gardens and filling this village with Hooray Henrys from down south."

"Customers from down south," François corrected.

"For you maybe, but not for me. What is your business model? Provide everything they need on site, I think. Before long all the people who come here to get away from it all will desert us. Then, as the house prices drop, people will move. Then, when you've picked the bones from this village, you'll probably buy up all the cottages as a full-blown holiday resort."

François hadn't thought that far ahead but it wasn't a bad idea. He thought it best not to mention it to Darryl just yet. "That's certainly one doom-filled way of seeing it. How many houses do you and your husband own?"

Liz scowled at him. "We own four."

"And you're worried. I can understand that. Allow me to give you a new perspective. Staff accommodation."

She looked confused but for once didn't interrupt him.

"The many staff members it takes to run a hotel like that won't live on site. We will be needing good quality lodgings for them. I don't see why we wouldn't give the lucky venues a year contract. A year's guaranteed income isn't to be sniffed at."

If she had been in a cartoon, pound signs would have flashed up in her eyes. He recognised her hunger to make money. Something he and Darryl shared. He'd been right to come to Liz first.

"Let's say I'm interested," she said.

It touched him that she had attempted to bargain with him. He had her on the line and was reeling her in. They both knew it.

"Of course, you'd probably have to ask your husband"

Liz reared up. "Never you mind about him. How would I go about applying?"

François picked up a faded pen from a selection and played with it, giving her a moment of apprehension before he struck.

"No point. If we get much more grief from the locals, I think Darryl will give it up as a bad job. We got refused in the pub tonight. Poor Darryl is at the end of his tether. We'll probably just carry on with the car park and build some flats. Sell them off cheap to make our money back."

"Flats? Cheap?"

"Yeah. It's a shame. We had some great plans, but what can you do?"

"You leave the locals to me," she said.

Chapter Nineteen

With nerves that were quite uncharacteristic, he climbed over the stile, into the field. His breath plumed like smoke in front of him as he stole across the frozen grass. The tarn lay covered in ice and reflected the morning sun, giving it a mirror effect. It was truly beautiful.

Darryl had snuck out before François had got up. Considering he owned the Hall, it had seemed a little galling that he had to creep about. He hadn't done that since he'd escaped the children's home to go into central London as a fearless teenager.

The poor old heron stalked around the shoreline at the opposite side. Food would be slim pickings today with everything under a sheet of ice, but it didn't seem to give up. Darryl had to admire its spirit. The sound of the icy grass crunching under foot made him whirl around.

"Morning. Fancy seeing you here."

Michael emerged from the wood. Even at the crack of dawn he still had model looks. Darryl watched him approach and enjoyed the view.

"Morning," Michael said, shyly.

"Shall we walk?" Darryl said. "It's too fucking freezing to stand around."

Michael nodded, and they set off on the circular path which traced the edge of the tarn.

"How have you been?" Darryl continued.

"Oh, you know. Not bad. I've started putting feelers out for work. It's coming up to the time when people want to sort their gardens out, so fingers crossed."

For the hundredth time, the guilt for what they had put Michael through overpowered him.

"How about you?" Michael asked.

Ever since they'd realised they were public enemies in the village, François and Darryl had avoided it like the plague. François seemed very confident that he could sort the situation, but Darryl tired of his schemes.

"Pretty good. We've nearly done all our bits for the site. The project manager will be coming soon. That's our cue to bow out."

Michael's body seemed to tense when he announced that. "Will you come back?"

"Yes, when they're done save the snagging. François wouldn't let anything open until he's gone over it with his beady little eyes."

Michael laughed. "I'm sure the crew fear him. You're lucky he's so good at his job."

Darryl glanced across. "Considering the way he's treated you, I'm surprised to hear you have anything decent to say about him."

Michael didn't return his look, preferring to focus straight ahead. "I don't bother with grudges, Darryl.

I'm not going to say you two haven't hurt me. I liked you both, a lot. But I'm a grown-up. Ignoring folk and whispering campaigns aren't my style. Which is why you've asked me for this early morning walk, isn't it?"

Darryl stopped. "What do you mean?"

"It's pretty obvious. You've had a week of cold shoulder from the village and want me to wave my magic wand to fix it."

He deserved these words but that didn't make them palatable. "Michael, this has all got out of hand. I know that François has his fair share of blame."

"That's putting it mildly," Michael said eventually.

Michael always seemed to consider everything he said. The mirror opposite to François. "There's a lot to François. Not many people see the decent guy underneath it all."

"I know," Michael replied. "If you could get across to him that you weren't impressed by this cold bitch side, you'd find life easier. But then, I suppose it comes in useful for you."

The last barb wounded Darryl. He had always blamed François' quick temper and little plans for any trouble they found themselves in. It came as a revelation to him that he was the puppet master of this. *Do I really use him for my own ends?*

Michael must have noticed his comments hit home. "Has no one ever said that to you?"

"People don't tend to tell me the truth these days. It's bad for business."

"What is it you want from me?" Michael asked.

Darryl exhaled. "I don't know. I'd hate for us to part on bad terms. I like you, Michael, very much."

"I like you too, but our lives are going to head off in different directions. François will drag you to Kenya pretty soon, and my next contract could be anywhere in the country."

They turned onto the road, and Michael set off toward the village. Darryl stopped.

"What's up?" Michael asked.

"I'll head along the shore. I don't want any grief."

Michael frowned. "Is it as bad as that? I didn't realise François had so much power over you."

Darryl leaned against the stile. "Whatever happens, Thorpe Hall is part of my business. A boycott from the villagers will impact it. I think it's best if François and I keep our heads down for the rest of our time here. Once we're out of the picture, they might go easy on the manager. I didn't want to upset anyone, Michael. That's not my game play."

"I get that, but you have."

"What can I do to make it up then?"

Michael seemed to give it some thought. Darryl loved the way his eyes scrunched up when he mulled something over. He had to fight every instinct not to lean forward and kiss him. "Tell you what. Call me a sucker for a sob story. Be at The King's at eight tomorrow night. I'll rally the troops. We'll have one more shot at resolving this. Put all the cards on the table."

Darryl nodded. "I appreciate this."

He climbed over the stile and onto the footpath. Michael stood on it, so his head peeked over the wall. "And, Darryl?"

Darryl turned.

"Muzzle François. He doesn't help matters."

* * * *

"I've a good mind to leave you at home," Darryl said, checking out his appearance in the bathroom mirror.

"Pah," François snorted. "Good luck with answering any questions that need actual facts."

Darryl couldn't deny it. François' capacity for organisation was second to none. But some of Michael's words had hit home as Darryl had made his way to the Hall that morning. François needed to be reminded of the pecking order. "Fine but only speak to me. I will handle things from there."

"Yes, boss. Whatever you say."

"There is the tone I wish to avoid, François. Don't push things."

"Fine. Best behaviour. Scout's honour."

Darryl frowned at him "You were a scout?"

"Of course not," François huffed, pushing him out of the door.

They set off to the pub. The church clock struck eight.

"Come on. Being late won't endear us to anyone."

They jogged the rest of the way and into the pub. To Darryl's astonishment, it was dead inside. He couldn't even see Michael. At first, he thought he had been set up, but refused to believe Michael would do that.

"I told you this would be a waste of time," François muttered. "I expect there was a riveting programme about Yorkshire railways on television."

"Shut up. I mean it." He walked up to the bar.

"Evening," Becky said before shooting a filthy scowl at François.

"Isn't Michael here?" Darryl asked. "We were supposed to meet him."

"Darryl," came a voice from behind them.

Michael approached. To his credit he didn't even falter when he saw François.

"I guess no one wanted to resolve things," Darryl said. "Thanks for trying. At least let me buy you a drink."

The gardener looked confused. "What are you on about? We're all in the function room."

Darryl felt a rush of apprehension. He had only really thought about seeing Michael again. Now he truly was walking into the lion's den.

"Come on," Michael said, holding his arm out to point the way. "I'm sure François can get the drinks. Becky, my usual and whatever these two are having. On my bill."

François would be apoplectic. Darryl quite enjoyed this confident version of Michael. He cared for François very much, but a few life lessons would do him no harm.

He followed Michael through to a room off from the main bar. About thirty people were sitting at tables. He saw Will and Andrew, James, Ed and Arthur, Mrs Turnbull, Liz Poole and the Holdsworths. The rest of the people he recognised to say hello to.

A whole community stared at him. One which had a collective scowl, meaning they were prepared to fight for where they lived. The shame that he should be the one to threaten this swept over him. Nodding at a few people, he sat down in the chair Michael offered him.

François came in, carrying a tray with three pints that he put down on the table in the centre of the circle. As usual, he didn't come across as particularly outfaced by the tension in the room. His confusion lay with the lack of an empty chair though. "Where am I to sit?" he asked Michael.

Michael pointed to a chair by the door. For a split second, François looked as though he were about to lose his temper. Credit to him, when he locked eyes with Darryl, he dutifully took his pint to the corner.

"Okay, everyone," Michael said. "I called you here to listen to what Mr Burlington has to say. He asked for this, by the way."

Darryl cleared his throat. He had done presentations to boards and spoken at large events, but they were nothing to this.

"Thank you all for coming. I wanted to speak to you to explain my intentions for Thorpe Hall. There has been a lot of talk in the last week, and I thought it best to cut through all that."

A few people shifted in their seats, but to his relief, he seemed to have the room.

"When I saw Thorpe Hall, I knew I could do something wonderful with it. At Burlington Hotels we pride ourselves on finding hidden gems and restoring them to glory. I truly want to do that again."

"What if we like being a hidden gem?" Mrs Turnbull said.

"Let him speak," Liz barked.

He could have sworn he saw a look exchanged between her and François, which made him feel nervous to say the least.

"Thank you, Mrs Poole. I understand change is nerve-wracking. But when the Hall went on the market, it was always going to be someone like me who bought it up. I want to help the economy of Napthwaite."

Christine Carrington sighed. "Suppliers from out of town. Guests damaging the local wildlife. You're going to kill this village. Don't try to fool us into thinking you don't know this."

Darryl shook his head. "I don't believe that, Mrs Carrington. We have helped locals start businesses in lots of the destinations we have opened hotels in."

"Let me guess," she countered. "Souvenir shops, local crafts and artisan chocolates? Am I right?"

"Does it make a difference?" Liz asked.

"I might have known you'd follow the pound signs," Christine muttered. "Those things are not what makes a community. If you turn Napthwaite into a theme park, house prices will skyrocket."

"And that's a bad thing, is it?" François said from the back.

Darryl scowled at him.

An agitated Rob Holdsworth glared at him. "Yes of course it is. Our kids will have to move away. The school will be the first to go, but then you'll probably build a spa on it. After that, the shops we need follow suit. The post office and the butchers. Queen Street will be full of expensive tatt."

He looked from one local to the other.

"That's the way of the world though. Everything is changing," Liz countered. "You all bugger off to the supermarket in Holton. Don't you think that impacts my business?"

"Liz. Even residents from Napthwaite need vitamins from time to time," Mrs Carrington retorted.

Will stood up. "You are killing this village and you think we will let you do that. You won't even be here. You and your lapdog will be off destroying another community. All you'll get is some bloody spreadsheet telling you how much money you're making."

To Darryl's horror, François stood. "You are just guilty because you made your father sell up. I think you should probably fix your own demons instead of expecting us to do it for you. You're the one dragging this village down, not us."

Will launched at him. Luckily Andrew grabbed hold of him before he made contact. "You vicious bastard," Will shouted.

Michael jumped between the two men in the blink of an eye. "Will, this isn't helpful."

Andrew forced Will down in his chair.

"He has a point though," Rob Holdsworth said, scowling at Darryl.

"Making money isn't a crime, Rob," Liz shouted in response.

"You're so fucking predictable, Liz," Rob's wife, Jenny, said.

François tried to move closer to Will. "Darryl has come here to speak to you all and you repay him by behaving like this."

Michael put his hand on François' chest. "Leave him be. You've said enough."

"François. Stop this," Darryl said.

But François wasn't for stopping. He batted Michael's hand away from him and tried to push past to get to Will.

"I said leave him," Michael snarled.

Michael shoved him away. François lost his footing and fell onto the chair, then onto the floor. He looked up, shocked.

"You will regret that."

Chapter Twenty

"I'm going to sue the arse off him," François ranted. He poured himself a large brandy. "See how he likes being someone's cell bitch for the rest of the year."

He had never been so humiliated in his life. Having to be helped up by Rob Holdsworth while the whole village howled with laughter at him had been too much. *Michael Fleming will pay for this.*

"You're giving me a headache. You couldn't keep your mouth shut, could you?"

"I know you think he's the best thing that's ever sucked your dick. But letting him get violent with me is too much. Would it kill you to show me a scrap of loyalty?"

Darryl drained his whiskey glass. "He did not get violent with you. I told you to let me handle it. As usual, you had to go in both barrels and caused mayhem."

"Are you saying this is my fault? I might have known."

"I'm saying that this is my company. It's time you remembered that."

François had heard enough. "Fine. Then perhaps I will take some leave. You can run your company by yourself."

He didn't wait for Darryl's response. Instead, he stormed out of the room, letting the door bang behind him. Standing in the hallway, he took in the dark wood panelling and the dated light fittings. He hated this building now. It was cursed.

Once in his room, he let the tears of frustration come. Everything had collapsed around him. He didn't want Darryl to hear him so thrust his face in his pillow and just let them fall.

His mother had always said that crying was the body's way of releasing the hormones a person needed to deal with whatever situation he found himself in. But François had no idea how to deal with this one.

Anyone with half a brain could see that Darryl and Michael shared more than just lust. What made it worse was François couldn't separate his feelings. He had loved Darryl ever since that first moment they had met on Compton Street, but he was so in deep with the persona he had created to please him that he had lost himself.

As for Michael, he desperately wanted to hate him, but his innocence and decency called to a part of François he had shut away many years ago. Maybe it would be a good idea to get some distance from them both.

What if my time with Darryl is coming to an end? What would I do?

Leaving them to their own devices would be a bad move. Michael would easily charm Darryl around to agreeing to whatever he wanted. François needed to think of another ploy.

He had a sleepless night. He hadn't been able to get comfortable and his mind wouldn't stop whirring. The bruise that had appeared on his arse was nothing compared to the damage that had been inflicted on his ego. Michael might be a saint, but he had gone too far.

To his amazement, there was a knock on his bedroom door.

"Come in."

Darryl entered. François' eyes widened when he saw him carrying a steaming cup of coffee.

"I thought you might like a drink in bed for a change."

François sat up. "What a treat," he managed. He tried to read the expression on Darryl's face but to no avail.

Darryl put the cup down on the side table and perched on the end of the bed. "How are you feeling this morning?"

"I couldn't sleep thanks to a rather impressive bruise that's appeared on my butt," he muttered. "I'm in agony if you must know."

"Want me to check it over for you?"

François narrowed his eyes. "We only play with others, remember," he said, echoing Darryl's words. "And somehow I don't think Michael will be up for playing nursemaid. Seeing as he caused it."

"Let's not start that again."

He and Darryl had never fought this much in the whole eight years put together. He hated this change in their dynamic.

"Are you still going to leave?"

François took a sip of his coffee. "I should, but let's face it, you haven't a fucking clue what is going on. The mess you would leave me to unpick would undo any rest I might grab for myself."

Darryl smiled. "That's true enough." He took the cup from François' hands and had a sip.

"Typical. You can't even let me have my drink in bed in peace."

Darryl winked and handed it back to him. "Last night did make me think though. We are going to cause some real damage to this place. Have we ever gone back to a destination and analysed our effect? I bet we haven't."

"Seeing as you've never given a shit before, no, we haven't."

Darryl got up, guilt making him restless. "Perhaps it's time we stopped acting like we have no responsibility."

"Fine, I'll get in touch with the managers. Find out a way to at least measure it."

Darryl sat on the window ledge. "Thanks. I'm lost without you. I think we should do something to support the communities."

François smoothed the duvet out. "I'm sure the board will be over the moon with that."

"Then I'll pay for it myself."

They sat in silence for a moment or two.

"I've been thinking about the idea I had about having this place as a home," Darryl ventured.

François had no intention of setting foot in Napthwaite once Thorpe Hall was up and running. He did not want Darryl having a permanent tie to this place. "Burlington Hotels owns this place, remember?

Why would they sell it off when it's on the verge of making a fortune?"

Darryl sighed. "It's just getting so repetitive." He stared out of the window again. "Maybe we could at least save the garden."

François studied Darryl's profile as he stared at the view which overlooked those fucking flowerbeds. He had seen him close deals and be so animated anyone would think the source of life flowed through him. "Jesus Christ," he grumbled. "Shall we let the guests all park on the green then? Will that stop those halfwits from moaning? Somehow I doubt it very much."

Darryl got up and walked over to the door.

"You're probably right. Come on, get cracking. If we get our heads down, we can at least get the opening orders sorted today."

He went out of the room, closing the door behind him. François sank onto the pillows. This whole situation had got out of hand. Darryl only wanted to save the garden so that Michael would be in their lives a bit longer. The next suggestion would be to personally oversee the work at the Hall. He could imagine it. What would happen to Kenya then?

Suddenly an idea came to him. He reached across to grab his phone, dialling the number for Bianca Cartwright. As the executive assistant to Cole Jackson, the second biggest investor in Burlington Hotels after Darryl, she wielded a degree of power in the London head office.

"François? What a lovely surprise. How are you?"

"I'm fine. Still stuck in the middle of nowhere in the frozen north."

"Poor baby," she laughed. "What can I do for you?"

"It's more what I can do for you."

He proceeded to tell her about Darryl's indecision about the site, the issues with the villagers and the gardens.

"Are you telling me that Darryl Burlington is getting worked up about some old shrubs?" she said.

"It's more the gardener who tends to those shrubs."

"Have you two been up to your old tricks again?"

Everyone in Burlington Hotels knew that Darryl and François generally picked up a lover or two in each location. The Board went so far as to see it as a bad omen if they didn't.

"It's different this time, B. He's gone all googly-eyed over him."

"Wow, he must be a knockout."

"Oh, he is," François said, ignoring the glow that kicked in even talking about Michael in this way. "Mr Perfect. I just don't want Darryl to throw this whole project away on a cheap fuck. I think he must be having a midlife crisis. Men get funny at his age."

"No, Cole will be livid. Thank you for telling me. I'll have to share this with Cole — you do know that."

François had thought about this. "Perhaps you could ask Darryl for a personal update on things? I know how much Cole hates Zoom calls. I'm sure he's within his rights to demand Darryl deliver it in person."

"You are a slippery little shit, aren't you?"

"It's the only way to survive, Bianca, *ma chérie*."

Chapter Twenty-One

François felt very pleased with himself as he wandered across the green. Things were coming to a close and he would be glad to get on that plane soon. Liz had been all over him when he'd gone in the shop to buy batteries. Not to have to try to make food from her poor selection of ingredients was also a relief. He wondered what he would be eating in Kenya.

Passing Michael's house, he frowned at the door open. The workmen had taken down the scaffolding so things must be completed. As he stared in, Michael appeared in the doorway.

"Oh, hello," François said.

"Staring in people's houses now? I'm sure there's a law against that."

François sighed. "I hadn't realised the work had finished. I wouldn't have forgiven myself if you were being burgled and I did nothing."

"I'm sure you would."

François started to move off. "Well, I'll bid you good day and maybe even goodbye."

Michael walked down to his gate. "Goodbye? Has Darryl finally done himself a favour and got rid of you?"

He looked so handsome, leaning on the gate. Dressed in sweatpants and a hoodie, he radiated sex appeal. François felt a stab of guilt at how he'd treated him, but he couldn't lose focus now. The chequered flag was in sight. "Michael, you put up a good fight and I'm impressed. But it's over."

"Come in for a second," Michael said, opening the gate.

Intrigued, he followed Michael down the path and into the small cottage. The work had been done well, but the place would need new everything. The carpets had been stripped out and the walls desperately needed decorating. Only a sofa and a chair remained.

"Looks like you'll be busy," François said. "The storm ruined everything."

"Has Darryl made up his mind what he's doing with the Hall?" Michael said, ignoring his attempt at small talk. "Is that why you're leaving?"

Straight to the point. François liked that. "Didn't he tell you? The board were understandably concerned about his dithering over the place. Very out of character. They called him down to London immediately to meet with them. Between you and me, they're not happy at all. Poor Darryl will be facing quite the grilling."

Michael shook his head. "I'm sure they came to that conclusion all by themselves."

François held his hands up. "I've been here the whole time. Even you can testify to that. My goodness,

Michael. You would blame me if the sun didn't come up in the morning."

Shaking his head, Michael scowled at him. "And what does it mean? Darryl being dragged down to the London?"

"It means the higher powers are keen to see this project through. They've asked me to get everything ready for the project manager to get cracking. They feel that Darryl is compromised. I doubt he'll even be back. We're all about Kenya now. A bit of sun will do us both good. Put this little episode behind us."

Michael sank down on the sofa. "That's it then? Business as usual."

François sat next to him. "Like I said. You put up a good fight, but it was only going to end one way. Don't be too downhearted. I'm sure there are plenty of people who need digging and things."

"Like you give a shit," Michael muttered. "Tell me one thing though, honestly."

"Go on. I'm always honest. It's a curse and a blessing."

"Why?"

François thought about this for a second. He couldn't possibly expect Michael to understand his relationship with Darryl. "Because I always play to win, Michael. Always have and always will do."

"Were you more bothered by my friendship with Darryl or that you showed me the person underneath all that bullshit?"

"For a manual worker, you can be very profound. I'll give you that."

Michael took hold of François' hands. "Stop. It's just you and me. I saw you. The poet. The thinker. The person who cares deep down. Why did you throw that away and produce this…this vicious bitch?"

François tried to pull his hands free, but Michael had a firm grip. "Take your hands off me."

"Not until you tell me. Why can't you let it go? Be a decent person."

A lump appeared in his throat, and he wanted to get out, but Michael blocked him. "Are you going to abduct me now? It would be quite fitting if you buried my body in those fucking gardens."

"If this is truly the last time we'll see each other, I want to know why you destroyed everything I worked for. I deserve that at least."

"Because…"

"Go on."

François stared him straight in the eyes. "Because you got too close. There. Are you happy now?"

"Too close to Darryl? He cares about you no matter what. Surely you can see that."

"Not just him. To me."

Michael looked shocked for a second. "To you? I thought you said you were in love with Darryl."

François thought he had nothing to lose. "It's possible to be in love with two people at the same time, you know. But that isn't how we play. It's only fun for me and Darryl. It's worked well all these years and I wasn't about to let you ruin it."

Michael moved closer. "That's ridiculous. We could all be together."

François shook his head. "No. You'd soon push me out. It's Darryl you're after. It's been him all along. Don't treat me for a fool."

In response Michael leant forward and kissed him. François desperately wanted to fight him off, but he couldn't resist the feel of their lips together. It was exactly like the night Darryl had lain ill in bed – the intoxicating presence of Michael reduced him to jelly.

They fell to the floor, a mass tangle of limbs. To feel Michael's muscular body close to him again made François give up to the moment. Something he never did. The heat of Michael's breath on his neck made his cock ache. He shrugged his jacket off and rolled Michael over onto his back. Their lips met again, harder and more passionately.

François pulled the zip down on Michael's hoodie and ran his hands inside. Straddling him, François unbuttoned his shirt and shrugged it off, letting it fall to the floor. Michael wrapped his muscular arms around François' slender body and gently manoeuvred him onto the floor so their naked chests touched. François let out a moan.

Michael kneeled over him, his hard cock pressing against his jeans. In no time, Michael wriggled out of his clothes. François kicked his shoes off and Michael dragged his jeans and boxers down.

Licking his lips, Michael went straight for the prize and sucked hard at François' erection. François let the waves of pleasure wash over him, the heat from Michael's mouth engulfing him. Running his hands through his hair, François watched Michael's lips sliding up and down his cock. God this man was hot and decent. A combination that made him irresistible.

Their lips met again, and François revelled in their cocks rubbing together. He massaged Michael's balls, running them between his fingers. Michael lay on his back, giving him full access.

François moved between Michael's legs, spreading them, and reaching for his cock. François took

Michael's full cock in his mouth. Michael gave a yelp and bucked his hips. François couldn't get enough and bobbed his head up and down, picking up speed. He'd had a taste of Michael and wanted more.

"Oh shit, François…"

But he ignored his warnings. It didn't take long. Michael grabbed his head and fucked his face. François grabbed at his balls and squeezed.

"Oh yeah," Michael shouted. He came hard, his orgasm filling François' mouth. Michael's body spasmed. François crawled up his body and kissed him.

Michael shoved him onto his back and took hold of his cock. Relaxing into the inevitable, François spread his legs. Michael was sucking and nipping at his balls. François moved his legs and Michael's tongue found his hole. François took over pulling at his cock as Michael explored his arse. His hole was wet enough for Michael to push a finger in. François relaxed his legs and rode the digit. Michael pushed François hand aside and resumed massaging his cock.

Just as Michael found his prostate, François could last no longer. He let out a cry as he came over Michael's hand and his own body. "Oh Jesus," he managed.

Michael sank to his side, and they lay there for a second. The blindness of passion subsided, and François realised he'd made a stupid mistake. Grabbing his boxer shorts. he wiped himself clean and began to put his jeans on.

"What are you doing?" Michael said.

"That was a mistake. The last one I will make with you, Michael Fleming." He shuddered as Michael ran his hand up his body. He might have been spent, but Michael's touch still gave him chills.

"Was it though? Neither of us could resist. François, think about this for a second."

He got to his feet and quickly put his T-shirt and jumper on. He needed to be out of there. "There's nothing to think about. It's over. We won't see each other again after today."

A deflated Michael smiled sadly. "One more for the road then, eh?"

Guilt overtook François and he sank down on the sofa. "Not like that at all. I just can't. I will admit that I have feelings for you, of course I do. But Darryl…"

Michael got up and pulled his sweatpants on. "Fine. I wasn't going to tell you because I thought I should wait and see what was going on at the Hall, but I guess you're right. It's over. I've been offered a contract at a big house in Devon. It's right on the coast, so it will be a challenge."

The guilt seemed to ease a little. François was genuinely happy that Michael had an option. Once the dust had settled on this deal, he wouldn't wish the man any long-term ill-will. Shoving his boxer shorts in his jacket pocket, he put it on. "That's wonderful. Really it is. I know you think I run on venom, but I do want you to be happy."

"I would have said no if there was a chance with the Hall."

"Wrong place, wrong time." He kissed Michael. "When do you go?"

Michael shrugged. "There's no point in unpacking my stuff really, is there? I might as well set off today."

"I will tell Darryl you said goodbye."

Michael stared at him, taking his face in. François wanted to get out of there as quickly as possible.

"I've never met anyone like you, François. I would wish you happiness. There's no point though. I honestly don't believe you would know what to do with it if it bit you on your arse."

François walked over to the door. "Despite what's happened, I hope things work out for you, Michael. Honestly I do." He didn't wait for an answer.

Darryl wouldn't be home until the next day and despite what was decided about the Hall, Michael would be long gone. All in all, it had been a good day. He would treat himself to a bottle of champagne he'd kept for a special occasion.

Humming a happy tune, he sauntered back to the Hall.

Chapter Twenty-Two

The dark winter night claimed another day as Darryl drove through the winding country roads. Napthwaite was a long way from a motorway, but he didn't mind that. It made a nice change to be off the beaten track.

He tried to contact Michael again, but the phone went straight to answer machine. Having already left two messages, he worried a third would sound desperate. He slammed on the brakes. A deer stood in the middle of the road. Seemingly unconcerned by his car, it slowly strode across. Darryl watched it in awe. A beautiful creature that seemed to know exactly where it belonged. He wondered if it lived in the woods by the tarn.

As it reached the wall, it stopped and looked at him. Darryl found himself smiling in response, making him feel totally ridiculous. The deer held his gaze. Suddenly the spell shattered as the lights from a car coming in the other direction lit the place up. The deer silently bolted. It cleared the wall and disappeared into the woods on the other side.

The oncoming car sped past, unaware of the moment it had just broken.

Darryl shrugged. There would be plenty of time to get to know the rest of the local wildlife. Flooring the accelerator, he set off towards the small village he had grown to love. He had news that would affect them all. He prayed all this nastiness would be gone as quickly as the deer over the wall.

Pulling up on the drive, he saw the gothic ramparts of the Hall shadowed by the last light of dusk. What a beautiful building. Instead of going inside, he got out and wandered around the perimeter of the building. An owl hooted in the woods over by Thorpe Tarn. The gardens were in pitch dark until he tripped the security light. The beds became illuminated, and he sat on a bench. It would be a crying shame to have this full of the latest fancy cars from industry bigwigs flocking to the country to find themselves amid overpriced wines and gourmet canapes.

Movement in the corner of his eye made him glance up at the building. François stood at the landing window like a modern-day Mrs Danvers.

Darryl had purposefully ignored his messages, letting him stew. He would be beside himself with curiosity. He couldn't prove it, but he would put his last million on François having something to do with him being called in front of the board. He had felt like a naughty child being summoned by the headmaster. He'd experienced that a lot in his youth.

The French doors to the kitchen opened and François came out. He rubbed his arms to evade the cold as he made his way over the gardens to where Darryl sat. "You made good time," he said. "Come inside. It's bloody freezing out here."

Darryl stared at the grounds around him. "I need to go into the village. Have you heard from Michael?"

François frowned. "No. Did you expect me to?"

Darryl shook his head. "I guess not."

"Aren't you going to tell me what happened?"

Getting up, Darryl stared into his eyes. "No."

Walking down to the village, he could see the houses with their lights on. Some had smoke coming out of the chimney. He had always thought beauty lay in far-flung destinations. He realised how wrong he had been.

The King's was half-full as Darryl made his way through the crowd to the bar. Ed and Arthur were leaning against the bar and scowled when they saw him come in.

"Okay, okay. I come in peace," Darryl said, holding his hands up. "I wanted a word with Michael."

Ed put his pint down on the bar noisily. "He's not here. His cottage is ready."

Darryl frowned. He hadn't noticed any lights on when he came past. "Thanks."

After fighting his way out onto the green, he walked over to Michael's cottage. It reminded him of the night of the storm. He had instinctively wanted to make things all right then. Not just for Michael, but the whole village. For a split second, he had been a member of a community. It had been a new sensation, one that he had enjoyed.

The cottage sat in silence as he banged on the door. The nerves jangled around his system. He knocked again but still nothing.

Mrs Turnbull came out of her house next door. "Oh, hello," she said. "What do you want?"

"Hello, Mrs Turnbull. I'm sorry if I disturbed you. I came to see Michael."

"He's not here."

"I can see that. I wondered if you had any idea where he is."

She folded her arms. "Whether I did or not, I wouldn't tell you. Can't the pair of you leave that boy alone? You've turned his whole world upside down."

Her piercing eyes could have ripped his soul apart, they made him that uncomfortable. "I understand that. I wanted to explain. I have so much to tell him."

"Isn't that why you sent that little accomplice of yours? I saw him creeping around yesterday," Mrs Turnbull said. "Next thing I know, Michael is handing me his keys. He's gone after some job in Devon. He's a lovely lad and you've driven him out. The first of many no doubt. I'm sure you have plans for my cottage in that nasty little mind of yours."

Without waiting for a reply, she went inside and slammed the door. As he stood on the doorstep, frozen by indecision, he realised he'd never actually been in Michael's house. He had no idea what kind of décor he would choose or the oddments that would be scattered around. What would they have told him about Michael?

But he's gone now. You left it too bloody late.

He walked up to the Hall slowly, the weight of missed opportunity lying heavily on his shoulders. Once inside, he went through to lounge where François had built a roaring fire.

"Next time we do an English project, make sure it's in the summer. It's so cold out there," Darryl said. He wandered over to the fireplace to warm himself.

"Did you find him?"

Darryl shook his head and sank down on the sofa. The book François had been reading fell on the floor. François went to snatch it, but Darryl picked it up. "Yorkshire poetry, eh? Don't tell me this place is getting under your skin too."

"Nothing of the sort," François said, sniffily. "I had an idea of using some in the marketing for this place."

"Good old François. Never off duty."

They sat watching the fire crackle for a second.

"Why did you go and see Michael yesterday?" Darryl said.

From the corner of his eye, he saw François' body tense. It was almost invisible, but Darryl had learned to read every little nuance of his movements.

"Who said I did?"

"Don't answer my question with a question. You know very well you can't do anything in this village without word getting out. A lesson you seem to refuse to learn."

François tried to get up, but Darryl took hold of his arm. "He will ring me back eventually. It's better that you tell me."

"For goodness' sake. I don't know what this village does to you. I'm glad we're leaving soon, and Stan can finish this bloody place."

The time had come. Darryl gestured to the sofa for François to resume his seat, which he did.

"Stan isn't coming, and Kenya is off."

François recoiled. He started to rub his hands together. "What are you talking about? Everything is arranged. I've booked the flights and sorted the hotel."

"Bianca is going to check it out. It's time she had a promotion from Cole's lackey."

François swallowed hard and ran his hands through his hair. "What are we going to do then?"

"We're going to be honest with each other. Why did you go to see Michael yesterday?"

"I didn't—"

"Enough. Mrs Turnbull told me you were sniffing around his house, and what happens next? He disappears. You're going to have to convince me you haven't been up to your old tricks."

This time François did get up and stalked across the rug to the fireplace. "Are you going to accuse me of murdering him now? Who the fuck have you come as? Hercule Poirot?"

For so many years Darryl had come to rely on François. A lump formed in his throat. "I know you tipped Bianca off. I also know you did a deal with Liz Poole for her to supply staff houses. James told me. We haven't even discussed where to house staff. What the fuck are you doing?"

François shrugged. "I wanted to keep you focused and get this shitshow over the line."

"By lying and cheating everyone? Including me?"

"Don't be so melodramatic. I've never done anything without your best interests at heart. You know that."

François staring defiantly at him made him question every conversation they had ever had. "You caused a man to be driven out of where he lives? You are unbelievable. Okay, I'll let you know the outcome of our little meeting. I know for a fact that Bianca has been ignoring your calls because I instructed her to."

"Enlighten me. Where are we heading to now?"

"We're not heading anywhere. They approved my proposal for this place. I'll admit I had to do it on the fly, seeing as you forced my hand. But contrary to your opinion, I'm still the captain of this fucking ship."

The colour had drained from François' face. "What are you talking about? What proposal?"

"Thorpe Hall will be the new headquarters of Burlington Hotels. We've been paying London prices for way too long."

"What? And where are we supposed to live? Will we be lodging with Mrs Turnbull?"

"I'll be going to the estate agents in the morning. For me. I'm sorry, François, but it's the end of the line. You've gone behind my back one too many times."

François recoiled as though someone had let a bomb off. He threw himself down at Darryl's knees. "Darryl—"

"I mean it. I can't do this anymore. I'm forty-two years old. You are a liar and a schemer, François. I will not have that in my life."

"But I only did it for you."

"I'm sure. I'll give you twenty minutes to pack your things. I can't spend another night under this roof with you."

François reached out for Darryl's hand which he quickly swiped out of the way. Even though he deserved everything that was coming to him, Darryl still felt sadness at the sheer terror on François' face.

"I love you, Darryl. I always have. Please don't do this."

"Will you stop at nothing to get your own way?"

Tears rolled down François' cheeks. "Please. We were fine before we came here. Darryl, I'm begging you."

"Twenty minutes, François."

Chapter Twenty-Three

Michael hadn't got a wink of sleep. New beds always did that to him. He missed his own bed that had been ruined in the storm. But he'd slept solidly when he'd been staying at the Hall. If that was the kind of bed Burlington Hotels had, he would have to become a customer.

He stared at the ceiling. That would be the only connection he would have to Darryl and François now. It had only been a few days, but he missed them, even François who showed such depth when he allowed himself to.

What a powerhouse he would be if he harnessed that energy properly.

Voices coming from downstairs meant his presence would be required soon. His friends had been good enough to let him stay indefinitely. Whiling away the morning in bed wouldn't show much gratitude, no matter how tempting it was.

After a long shower, he threw on some clothes and made his way downstairs, trying to trick himself into a good mood.

"Good morning to you."

Michael smiled shyly. Andrew and Will were entwined on the sofa, their legs resting on Hardeep's lap. "I'm a bit late. Sorry, guys."

Will extracted himself from Andrew's clutches. "Coffee first, then breakfast?"

"Coffee would be great. But don't go to any trouble with food. Just a bit of toast will be good."

"Go and sit down over there," Will said, shooing him with a tea towel.

Michael sat in the chair next to the others. Hardeep massaged Andrew's feet. "No work today, Andrew?" he asked.

"Nope. Took a day off. The weather is supposed to be nice today. I thought I'd take Sally out on the hills. Get rid of that belly."

Sally, Andrew's black Labrador, raised her head.

"On her or you?" Will shouted through from the kitchen.

"Hilarious," Andrew replied.

"I'm on a break," Hardeep said. "If you were wondering."

"Looks like a long one," Will added.

"I'm sure Napthwaite can hang on a little longer for their electricity bills," Hardeep retorted.

"Have you—?" Michael started, then stopped. He wasn't sure if he should ask where Hardeep had delivered to.

Do they have some kind of Hippocratic Oath, like doctors?

"Been to the Hall?" Hardeep said, with a kindly smile, clearly reading the expression on his face. "Yes. I have."

"And?"

"There's trouble there."

Will came into the room and handed Michael a steaming hot cup of coffee. He sat on the arm of the chair.

"Go on then," Andrew said. "Don't leave the poor guy in suspense."

"Okay. When I got there, Darryl was just staring at the gardens. It was bloody freezing this morning, but he wasn't for moving. Turns out François is gone. Darryl threw him out last night."

All eyes fell on Michael. The news was unexpected to say the least. He shifted uncomfortably in his seat. "I don't know why you're all looking at me. I was upstairs the whole time."

"What the hell has François done to finally make him see sense?" Will asked.

"I didn't think it was my place to pry. Tell you what though, he hasn't had a wink of sleep. Looked rough as anything."

Worry for Darryl bubbled over inside Michael. He also worried for François. Not that he deserved it. Without Darryl, he was nothing. Where would he go in the middle of the night?

"Good bloody riddance. One down, one to go," Will said sniffily.

"That's a bit harsh," Michael replied.

"You think? Neither of them did anything good in the whole time they were here."

"Not true. They put the villagers up in the storm," Andrew said.

"Except that," Will conceded.

Michael's head was swimming. "I'm going to go," he said, getting up. "I need to see Darryl and find out what's happened."

"Hang on there," Will said. "Have you forgotten how they just dropped you? Leave it be, Michael. Do yourself a favour for once."

Michael had already put on his jacket. His heart told him what he had to do. In the same way it had told him not to go with the job in Devon. He had spent years watching life pass him by. Now he had a chance.

Andrew got up. "I think you're a fool going after them, but we all do stupid things for love." He glanced over at Will and Hardeep.

Michael opened the door and set off out into the cold winter's air.

"Michael." Will's head poked out of the doorway.

"What?" He tried to hide the impatience in his voice.

"Don't make it too easy for that little shit, François. If anything does happen there, you need to show him who's boss."

"Oh, I've finally got his number. Let's see what I can make of him."

Walking through the village, Michael felt sure staying had been the right decision. No matter what happened with Darryl or François, this was home now. He had no idea how he would earn money, but he had a suspicion word of mouth would find him something. He had gone from newcomer to hero in the last few weeks — he had every faith that the village would care for him.

"Hello, Michael."

He glanced up to see Mrs Turnbull waving madly from her garden gate. Liz Poole with her ever-present scowl, stood next to her.

"Hello, Mrs T."

"I thought they'd scared you off," she shouted.

"No such luck," Michael laughed. "I couldn't leave the best neighbour in England."

She blushed and waved him away.

"Liz," he said, nodding.

She smiled sweetly and turned back to Mrs Turnbull. Who knew what stories they were sharing? He reached the Hall. In the dark wintery afternoon, the only light on was in the kitchen. Instead of going to the big wooden door, he cut around the side of the building.

Darryl sat on the bench in the garden, looking lost in thought. He must have been out here for hours if he'd been there when Hardeep had delivered his mail.

"You'll catch your death out here," Michael said.

Darryl's head sprang up. He stared at him as though he were a ghost. "Michael?"

"The very same."

Darryl leapt off the bench. Dashing over to where Michael stood, he threw his arms around him, holding him so tight, he could barely breath. "Oh God, what are you doing here?"

"Can't I pay a friend a visit?"

Darryl kissed him. With feelings he couldn't even identify, Michael returned the kiss. A mix of relief, passion and fear all swirled around inside him. He never wanted the kiss to end, but eventually they broke apart.

Beaming, Darryl led him to the bench where they sat down. Still clutching each other's hands as if letting go would spoil the moment.

"I thought you'd gone to Devon," Darryl managed.

"Nah," Michael said. He entwined his fingers around Darryl's. "I heard they had mild winters and dry summers. Where's the fun in that? I thought you were going to Kenya."

Darryl rested his head on Michael's shoulder. "I've put it off for a few months."

Michael frowned. Nothing seemed to stay the same with this man. What scheme did he have planned now? "And?"

Darryl laughed and raised his head. "Look behind you."

Almost scared at what he would see, Michael turned. All that greeted him was the Hall. Standing firm as it had done for hundreds of years. "What?"

"The new headquarters of the Burlington Hotel Group."

Turning to Darryl, he searched his face for any sign of a joke. "Are you being serious?"

"Hundred percent. I met with the board and suggested we move everything up here. We pay an absolute fortune for our offices in Kensington. They're that old, they're collapsing around our ears. It's a waste of cash. The idea came to me when I was driving down. It's so much cheaper to operate from a place like this. Plus, I can guarantee you these gardens will be the centrepiece. I want everyone to talk about them."

Tears pricked at Michael's eyes as he thought how pleased Matthew would be. "I can't believe it."

"I'll need your help though. I know fuck all about plants."

"Are you sticking around then?"

Darryl nodded. "I'm sure I can find somewhere to lay my head. I'm resting my passport for a bit. I told them I would oversee the move and get everything set up. The last thing they want is for me to burn out."

Suddenly the heavens opened, and they dashed for the kitchen door. Giggling like children, they made it inside staying relatively dry.

"Ignore the mess," Darryl said sheepishly. Cups filled the sink and coffee had been spilt around the machine.

They sat at the dining table. Michael reached for his hand again. "What made you decide all this? It's a hell of a U-turn."

"The drive to London gave me time to get everything clear in mind. What I want. Thinking I had lost you made me miss everything about you, Michael. Your touch, your laugh and your smile."

Michael kissed him. "I missed you too."

"What do you reckon? There'll be a few jobs for villagers and plenty of people wanting to live here. Do you think I'll be forgiven by Napthwaite?"

"With a personal recommendation from everyone's favourite gardener, you should be okay."

Darryl smiled. "And do I have that?"

"You have whatever you need, Darryl," Michael replied. "I have never felt like this about someone before."

"Show me."

Chapter Twenty-Four

With a hunger, Darryl pulled Michael's T-shirt over his head. The break in their kiss didn't last long. Their mouths smashed together again as Darryl threw the clothing onto the chair in the corner.

The bed lay waiting. Darryl desperately needed a naked Michael in his arms. Running his hand down his taut chest, he found his waistband. Quickly undoing the buttons on his trousers, he slid his hand inside. Michael groaned as Darryl palmed his cock over his boxers.

Darryl pushed Michael away. "Fuck this messing around," he said with a grin.

He undid his shirt and threw it in the corner. Michael licked his lips and let his own trousers drop to the floor. In a matter of seconds, the rest of their clothes joined the pile. Collapsing on the bed, Darryl wrapped his legs around Michael's waist. He grabbed hold of Michael's muscular shoulders and their cocks rubbed together. He needed to feel so close to him that no one would know where he ended and Michael began.

They rolled over on the huge bed. Darryl straddled Michael, who grabbed his arse cheeks and dug his nails in. Michael's cock grazed against Darryl's hole. He never thought he would have this again. He closed his eyes and revelled in the closeness of Michael.

His cock leaked onto Michael's taut stomach. Darryl moved up Michael's muscular body. Michael opened his mouth and Darryl plunged his cock inside. Holding on to the headboard, he let Michael get used to it as he slowly bucked his hips.

Staring down at Michael sucking turned him on violently. With his free hand, Darryl grabbed Michael's hand. He picked up the pace and fucked Michael's mouth. God, it felt good.

Then he pulled out. Confusion fluttered across Michael's face, but Darryl simply winked. He spun around on the bed, so Michael had full access to his arse. He leant forward and took Michael's cock in his mouth. At the same time, Michael lightly licked his hole. The stimulation sent electricity up his spine, making him suck harder.

Michael grabbed Darryl's cheeks again. Once again, he drove his tongue over his hole. Darryl could barely focus on returning the favour. *Damn, he's good at this.*

Unable to wait any longer, Darryl got off the bed. He grabbed condoms and lube from his washbag. Michael made to get up, but Darryl rested a hand on his chest. After everything he had put Michael through in the last few weeks, this was the least he could do. Slowly he rolled the condom over Michael's throbbing dick. Michael moaned as Darryl lightly traced his fingertip over his balls.

Staring into Michael's expectant eyes, he squeezed lube onto his fingers. Michael shifted as he ran the liquid over his cock and slowly massaged. Running his lube-covered fingers over his own hole, he couldn't wait much longer.

Once again, he straddled the handsome man below him. Instead of letting his cock graze over him, he reached behind and guided it inside him. Normally he liked a lot more preparation time. Tonight, however, he wanted him so badly he didn't care. Ignoring the pain, he slid down Michael's dick.

They both let out a moan at the same time as he reached the base. He sat for a second to allow his body to get used to the invasion of Michael's solid cock. Michael reached for his hips. Darryl enclosed his hands over Michael's. Then he started to move. Slowly at first, giving himself time to savour every nuance.

Michael grabbed Darryl's cock as he sped up. He moved up the length of Michael, almost letting him free before crashing back down. His body burned with sensation as he repeated it time and again.

Tucking his feet under Michael's thighs, he rode him for all he was worth. Sweat poured off him, his cock standing proud in Michael's fist.

"Oh God, that feels good," Michael cried out.

Darryl was close to coming. He tried to bat Michael's hand away, but Michael held firm.

"Come," he commanded.

Unable to do anything else, Darryl ground his hips as he came hard. Michael expertly drained every drop out of him. He gently pushed Darryl off and got out from underneath him. Keeping Darryl on all fours, Michael pushed his cock inside. His heart rate still all over the place, Darryl submitted to being fucked.

Michael pounded him. It seemed that all the pent-up anguish and aggression of the last few weeks was coming out in sheer primal instinct.

"Oh fuck, Darryl. I'm coming." His body convulsed and he collapsed on top of him.

Once he'd pulled out and disposed of the condom, Darryl went in search of a towel. In the en suite, he cleaned himself up before coming into the bedroom. Michael lay on the bed looking absolutely perfect.

"Fuck. I needed that," Darryl said. He slid in next to Michael, resting his head on his chest. Michael's arm closed around him, the heat of the man instantly giving him comfort.

They lay there for a minute or two. Darryl marvelled at how complete he felt next to someone he was probably falling in love with. *Falling in love?* It was probably true, but things were a bit new for all that.

"I could fall in love with you," Michael whispered into his ear.

Darryl snuggled into him. It was like Michael could read his mind. "Then why don't you?"

"Isn't there an elephant in the room we need to discuss first?"

Leaning his head up, he stared into Michael's eyes. "What?"

"Where's François?"

Darryl could just imagine the outrage if François got wind that they had described him as an elephant. "Ah, François." He extracted himself from Michael's arms and plumped a pillow up. "Turns out he was playing us both," he said. "He told the board I was going to throw this place away because of you."

"He told me you were never coming back."

"The little shit," Darryl said bitterly. "I rumbled him and threw him out last night."

Michael sat up. He seemed to be genuinely concerned. Once again, Darryl marvelled at the goodness in Michael Fleming.

"How did that go?"

The guilt that had been eating away at Darryl returned. "Bloody awful, if I'm honest. He even told me he loved me. I've never met someone who could lie so easily. I used to think that an essential part of us doing business. When it's aimed at you, it's not so funny."

It hadn't been a day, but Darryl missed François. He tried to push it out of his mind. He lay naked in bed with a man who could give him everything. The future would be different and that was fine.

"You think that was a lie?" Michael said.

The statement took Darryl by surprise. "What?"

"François is obviously in love with you and you him."

The conversation had taken a direction that Darryl didn't like. He reached for Michael's hand, but Michael moved it away.

"What are you saying?" Darryl asked.

"I want you to be honest."

Darryl thought about his feelings for François. For years he had forced them into the box of work and sex. "It would never work. François is all about making cash. I'm ready to step off the carousel."

To his surprise, Michael burst out laughing. "The pair of you are ridiculous. You both do what you think the other wants instead of actually asking. I can't understand how you can work so well together when you barely know each other."

"When did you get all wise?" Darryl muttered.

Michael cuddled up next to him. "When I found things I wanted to fight for."

"Fuck, I'm confused."

"With what?"

"I'm falling for you, that's a given. But yes, you're right, I do love him. I can admit it now."

Michael ran his hands over Darryl's body. "It's not me you should be admitting it to."

"After the way he's treated you, are you honestly saying I should rehire him?"

Michael shook his head. "I'm saying you should get him back on different terms. There is a decent person inside François Vernier. I've seen him and he needs setting free. But it's a two-man job. I'm up for it if you are."

Realisation finally dawned. "Are you saying the three of us?"

Michael nodded. "This is Napthwaite, after all."

Chapter Twenty-Five

"You're lucky it's out of season. Are you staying tonight too?"

François sat in the chair watching the afternoon slip into evening. The dark clouds swirling above the valley matched his mood. He nodded.

"I'd better bring you some things then. I presume you don't want to be seen."

François grimaced at Liz standing in the doorway. "Just some bread and cheese, please."

"Maybe try to get some sleep. You look like shit."

He could imagine how awful he looked. He had arrived at Liz's door as soon as Darryl had thrown him out. The last bus had long since departed and he had nowhere else to go. Luckily one of her holiday lets was free, and she'd let him stay. She'd charged him an extortionate sum, but François couldn't very well barter. Deep down, he knew he deserved it.

He hadn't had much rest. Knowing Darryl was just up the road made it impossible. From the bedroom window, he could see Michael's cottage. It sat in darkness, so he must have gone to Devon.

"It can't be as bad as all that," Liz said.

Usually, François detested crying in front of people but he couldn't stop it. The tears ran down his face. "I'm a toxic person. Darryl is right, I should disappear. For everyone's sake."

Liz came across the room and crouched at his feet. She put her hand on his leg. François was inordinately proud of himself that his flinch was barely visible.

"Hey now. That's no way to talk. Sometimes we do things that we think are right and it's a hell of a wake-up call when we realise they aren't. Believe me, I am the queen of bad decisions."

François appreciated her attempt to make him feel better.

"Darryl might change his mind. You never know," she continued.

"I haven't heard from him all day. It's hopeless. I'll get the bus to Leeds tomorrow."

"Then what?"

"I'll think about that on the bus. The farther I get away from this place, the clearer my head will be."

Liz got up and adjusted the knees on her saggy leggings. "Keep telling yourself that all night if you want, love. It won't make it true."

The tears welled up again. "What the hell else am I supposed to do? Michael has gone to Devon and Darryl has banished me from the kingdom."

Liz looked lost in thought for a second.

François scowled. "Any suggestions would be gratefully received right about now," he snarled.

But Liz just smiled. "I'd best get back. Why don't you get some sleep? Honestly you do look quite bad."

* * * *

Eventually François had dozed off. He had been in a dead sleep when the sound of frantic knocking cut through his dreams. Dazed, he lay on the sofa, summoning the energy to answer.

The noise of keys in the door made him leap up but his feet got caught in the blanket and he fell to the floor. Just at that moment, Liz entered the room, followed by Darryl and Michael.

François kicked the blanket away and jumped to his feet. "What is the meaning of this? How dare you just walk in here?"

"I can walk where I like. I own the place remember?" Liz reminded him.

"I could sue you for invasion of privacy," François fired back.

"Oh, chill out. You asked for a suggestion. I brought you two," Liz said, sauntering past Michael and Darryl. She stopped and turned to Darryl. "A weekend away in one of your fanciest hotels should call us quits."

He smiled sweetly at her. "Consider it done."

She patted him on the shoulder before walking out, banging the front door behind her.

François looked from Michael to Darryl and back to Michael. "I thought you were in Devon."

"Made it as far as Andrew's."

His bashful grin made him so perfect. François wanted to grab hold of him right there. But the scowl coming from Darryl told him that would be a very bad decision.

"And Darryl? Don't tell me, you need me to come and work the coffee machine."

Darryl sat down on the sofa. "Go on then," he said looking at Michael. "Show me."

François turned to Michael. "Show him what?"

Michael moved across the room and took hold of François' hand. It took him by surprise and he stepped back.

"What are you doing?"

"I said that behind this bullshit there is someone vulnerable and decent."

Michael moved closer to him. This time François let him. His heart was pounding and he could sense Darryl watching him intensely. All he'd ever wanted was to open his heart to him. Now the moment was finally here, he wasn't sure if he could go through with it.

Michael wrapped his arm around his waist and François leaned into his chest. Now he could see Darryl.

"Is it true? You love me?"

François met his gaze. "I think I'm in love with both of you."

Darryl glanced up at Michael and got up from the sofa. He came over to them and wrapped his arms around both men.

"We were going to talk to you about that."

* * * *

As François dashed through the door, Darryl and Michael were already sitting up in bed. François lay the tray down on the bed and dashed over to the window. Throwing open the curtains, he bathed the bedroom in sunlight. Darryl and Michael winced.

"Bloody hell, François," Darryl groaned. He struggled to get under the duvet, almost upending the tray.

"Don't be so dramatic," François said. He grabbed the tray and set it on the dresser. "It's a beautiful day. We should enjoy it." He looked around the room. An empty bottle of champagne was upended on the bedside table and another lay at the foot of the bed.

"We enjoyed the night," Michael said, rubbing his eyes. He took the coffee François offered him. He sniffed the cup. "Wow. A couple of these babies and I'll be right with you."

François winked at him. He gave Darryl a drink and sat down on the side of the bed with his.

"I was having a think downstairs," he began.

Darryl flopped his head back on the pillow. "Oh no. This is never good."

Michael nudged him with his shoulder. He cast François a glance that made his spine shiver. He was on his side.

"Hear him out," Michael chided. "He's a very creative man."

"Thank you, Michael," François said. He turned to Darryl, resting his hand on his chest. "I was thinking. We should get the Kenya gig back on."

This seemed to pique Darryl's interest. He glanced to Michael before looking back at François.

"I'm listening," he said.

"Just think of it. Us three in Africa. We could do a safari."

François sat back, feeling very pleased with himself. But Darryl was frowning.

"And what's Michael supposed to do while we're touring hotel sites?" Darryl asked.

François sipped his coffee. "I had another thought. Why not bring Michael in as Director of Estates? We do the inside, he does the outside."

Darryl grinned. He grabbed François by the waist and pulled him close.

"Darryl. My coffee," François wailed.

"*Darryl. My coffee,*" Darryl mimicked. He kissed François hard on the lips. "I love your schemes when they work for me."

François beamed. It was true. He loved his schemes but now he had something real and tangible to put them to work on. François felt as though his heart could burst.

They both stopped kissing and turned to Michael.

"That is if you want the job," Darryl said.

For a second, Michael was immobile. François got the fear that he had gone too far again. Michael might not want him organising every part of his life.

Then a huge grin spread across Michael's face. "Of course I want the job. Let's travel the world and create shit."

He launched himself at the other two. Laughing they squirmed until they got into a comfortable position. François was in the middle with his face on Michael's chest and Darryl's arm slung over his waist.

Darryl and Michael kissed above his head before pulling away and nuzzling François' hair.

"This is nice," Darryl said.

"I…" François started then stopped.

"What?" Darryl said.

"Nothing."

"Go on," Michael said, kissing his head softly.

"I feel safe," François said.

Darryl pressed his body close to him. The heat from him sent shockwaves up François spine.

"So do I," Darryl said.

Michael too pressed closer, running his hand over François' hip and on to Darryl. "So do I," he whispered.

They hugged tightly.

**Want to see more from this author?
Here's a taster for you to enjoy!**

Two Tribes: Fool's Gold
Kristian Parker

Coming March 2023

Excerpt

Hi how r u?

Good thanks, u?

Good, too :0)

I like your profile. You're a hot guy.

So are you. What brings you to Manchester?

Liam Moseley glanced out of the window of his small flat. The rain pelted down as usual, but no one expected anything different from summer in Manchester.

His phone buzzed again.

Here for work. You live here?

All my life. Can't you tell by the pale skin?

His flat might have been a nondescript one-bedroom box, but he loved it. He'd made it as homely as he could. Growing up with a mother like his, he hadn't lived in any one place for very long, so it had meant the world to him when he could afford his own place.

A notification came through.

I think you're very attractive.

Thank you. Where are you from?

He put on his jacket. Harry would be here soon. They had some jobs to do today before heading to his boss, Jonny Wellingham's, house.

A buzz sounded.

Roma.

Must be a bit different to Manchester. What you doing here?

He needed to wrap this up before his day began. He'd only gone on the dating app to pass the time while he waited. Usually he would be on his PlayStation, but he didn't have time to get into that.

Searching for hot pale-skinned men? :0)

Usually on these apps, they got straight down to business, asking measurements and preferences. Having a bit of banter with someone made a nice change.

That your type then?

Putting his cigarettes, phone and keys into his pocket, he left the flat. Liam had always been a loner — he could feel out of place in a crowded room. He wandered up to the main road. Harry would pick him up there, meaning it was time to put his game face on.

His phone vibrated in his pocket again.

It is now.

This guy was a joker.

Handy that. My type is fit Italians. But I've got to go to work now, sorry.

He liked to keep his life separate and wanted to get into the zone of being a Wellingham Boy, a member of the gang who controlled Manchester. Gay boys were not welcome in that fake family. Jonny had made that abundantly clear over the years.

A black BMW came up the road and stopped right in front of him. The passenger door opened and Harry sniggered at him.

"You'll be picking up trade standing there. Get in."

Liam rolled his eyes and jumped into the car. As Jonny's right-hand man, Harry had seen it all. A black man in his early forties, he'd been with Jonny probably longer than Liam had been alive. He'd had his fair share of problems over the years, but Jonny had always protected him, something that Liam respected. Jonny might scream at his minions for anything under the sun, but God help anyone else who did.

"Where first?" Liam asked.

"The Hawaiian," Harry replied. "We need to pick up some cash."

The Hawaiian Paradise, one of Jonny's brothels, sat on the edge of the city centre. A rough old spot, most of Manchester had heard of it. Jonny hadn't spent any money on the dive in donkey's years, but he worked on the principle that horny men leaving pubs didn't really care about interior design.

Another message came in. Glancing at Harry, who seemed focused on the road, Liam slipped his phone out.

All work and no play. Don't you English think that is a bad thing?

He had a point. *I get plenty of play*, Liam replied.

"Who's that?" Harry asked. "Some bird?"

Liam looked out of the window at the ring road. So many blocks of flats were being thrown up. Jonny had considered investing but had spent the cash on more stock to offload to Manchester's party crowd instead. Jonny Wellingham only cared about profit.

"Something like that," Liam replied.

It felt quite cosmopolitan to be messaging someone from Rome. He'd barely left Manchester but one day, when he saved up enough money, he dreamt of just taking off. His brother, Shaun, had done that and had the time of his life...and ended up in Blackpool.

They drew up outside a kebab shop, a discreet sign above a doorway next to it the only indicator that customers had found their destination. It might not look like anything from the road, but it, along with three other brothels and the fact that he had Manchester's drug supply sewn up made Jonny an absolute packet. Had done for years.

They got out of the car and headed up the stairs to the room at the top that served as a waiting area. It contained a nervous-looking man in his early forties. who stared at them in terror.

"Relax, sunshine," Harry said. "Just here to see the management."

The visitor looked away, chewing on his lip.

Harry shook his head at Liam as they went through one of the doors that led off the main area.

The manager of the place, Deb, sat at the desk in the combined office, staff room and store cupboard room, frowning at her computer. This dissolved into a grin when she saw them. "Who do we have here?" she said. "Dumb and dumber. What can we do for you?"

Harry sat on the old sofa. "Came for some cash," he said. "What else?"

Deb patted him on the arm. "You know, you could have anything you wanted. Mates' rates."

"I'll bear that in mind," Harry replied. "But today, we need to take Jonny some money. You know how much he loves it."

Deb sighed and got up. In her mid-thirties, she'd worked her way up to managing The Hawaiian. Liam had known her ever since he'd started running with Jonny a decade ago.

"And here's our cute little Liam," she said, pinching his cheek. "That baby face could make a woman want to corrupt it."

"Never mind all that," Harry said. "You've got a punter outside. He looks like he's about to scarper as well."

Deb shrugged. "Gina is running late. I've told her about letting them run on, but she's such a professional. Everyone comes for Gina, apparently."

Liam burst out laughing. "We should put that on the sign outside."

Deb produced a bag of notes from the safe under her desk. She handed it over to Harry, who regarded it with disdain.

"This is a bit fucking light, isn't it?" he asked.

"I know." Deb shrugged again. "Business has been pretty shit. Don't be blaming me."

Harry put the bag inside his coat. "He won't be happy."

"Well, maybe if he spent some money on this place, he would get a better return." Deb sniffed. "Most of the rooms have damp and the mattresses... Well, let's not go into it."

It would be a brave man who would tell Jonny how to run his business. Liam left that to Harry. He had been on the receiving end of way too many screaming rants to stick his head above the parapet.

"Right, we're off," Harry said, getting up. "Can someone give that poor guy a fucking blowie in the next hour? We clearly can't afford to watch him leg it."

Deb huffed. "Fine. I'll do it myself."

They went out into the room. Luckily, the man still sat there.

"Right, sunshine," Deb said. "It's your lucky day. You got the boss."

His face lit up.

"We'll leave you to it," Harry said.

Liam followed him down onto the street, where a traffic warden circled his car.

"Don't even think about it," Harry said to him. "Wellingham business."

The traffic warden leapt away from the car as though it would explode at any second. "Oh...fine...don't do it again," he stammered before scuttling off down the street.

Harry shook his head and they got in.

"Why do you think business is down?" Liam asked.

"Fuck knows," Harry replied. "But it'll be a bloody headache for us, no doubt."

With Harry focusing on weaving through the city centre traffic, Liam quickly checked his phone. He had another message.

Maybe we should play sometime?

The picture of this guy set all Liam's emotions running wild. In his early thirties, he had raven-black hair and olive skin. He wore his hair slicked back and stared into the camera as though he owned the world. That kind of arrogance made Liam weak at the knees.

Anytime.

Harry's phone made them both jump as it rang. He had it linked to the in-car system, so the speakers kicked into life with Tina Turner's *Simply the Best*.

"Speak of the fucking devil," Harry said, clicking the Answer button. "What's up, Jon?"

"Who've you got with you?"

"Just our Liam."

"Right, I want you at the house now," Jonny commanded. His abrasive Mancunian accent always sounded like he was ready to lay into someone.

"What's up?"

"I'll tell you when you get here. Pick up Deano on your way."

The phone went dead.

Silence hung in the car for a second.

"Sounds ominous," Liam said.

Harry sighed. He turned the car around and they sped off towards Salford where Deano lived. Liam hated Deano and Deano hated Liam. He had joined the gang a couple of years ago and made it perfectly clear he had no respect for anyone, including Jonny. He only wanted the cash and the excitement. A dangerous combination.

They got to his house in record time. A very handsome lad, he'd covered most of his body in tattoos in an attempt to come across as hard. His baby face always let him down so he'd created a personality far more ugly.

Him leaping into the back of the car flooded it with the scent of cheap aftershave.

"Fucking hell, Deano," Harry complained, winding the window down. "You earn enough to buy something that won't strip fucking paint."

"You don't know anything about style," Deano muttered. He swatted Liam on the head. "All right, gayboy? I bet you've got all the aftershaves at home."

Liam ignored him. Deano always called him that. At first, he'd denied it, but it only served to encourage Deano more, so now he just let it slide.

"The boss is in a shit mood," Harry said. "So if you could be a bit serious, I'm sure we'd all appreciate it."

Deano settled into his seat, sparking up a cigarette. "He's always in a shit mood."

"An even shitter mood," Liam piped up.

"What's his fucking problem this time?"

Harry shook his head. "No idea, but he wants us all there pronto."

"You'd better put your foot down then, Harold," Deano said.

Liam glanced at Harry. He had annoyance written all over his face. They had spoken about Deano before and Harry had tried to get Jonny to bin him, but he worked hard and had absolutely no limits. Two things that Jonny Wellingham valued highly.

They carried on in silence. Liam sneaked a look at his phone. A message had come in from Marco.

Name the time and place. I'll be there.

He smiled to himself. It would have to wait until they dealt with whatever had got up Jonny's arse. But once he'd finished for the day, he might treat himself to meeting the handsome Italian.

What harm could it do?

About the Author

I have written for as long as I could write. In fact, before, when I would dictate to my auntie. I love to read, and I love to create worlds and characters.

I live in the English countryside. When I'm not writing, I like to get out there and think through the next scenario I'm going to throw my characters into.

Inspiration can be found anywhere, on a train, in a restaurant or in an office. I am always in search of the next character to find love in one of my stories. In a world of apps and online dating, it is important to remember love can be found when you least expect it.

Kristian loves to hear from readers. You can find his contact information, website details and author profile page at https://www.pride-publishing.com

PRIDE
PUBLISHING

Sign up for our newsletter and find out about all our romance book releases, eBook sales and promotions, sneak peeks and FREE romance books!